THE ALPHA FILE

HUNT FOR A KILLER

JONATHAN M EDMANS

Table of Content

CHAPTER 1

The morning sun rose over Beijing; there was no cloud in the sky, a perfect day, a perfect spring day for an escape. Lin Kang, or to be more precise, Colonel Lin Kang of the second bureau of the Ministry of Security of the People's Republic of China. Kang, in his early fifties with greying hair and features that could be said to be hawk-like, his pointed nose, the set eyes, the mouth that when closed seemed to hold everything, at that moment he was standing by his window, his long fingers around a teacup.

Today was the day of the reckoning, the day when his career would come to a successful end when he would leave the prison known as the People's Republic of China, but also leave behind another past, a past that, if it caught up would destroy him and all that he had worked for in smashing the inner core of the political snake that he had worked in since he was 18. His mind went back to a flat in 1989; he was seventeen, it was June, and he was in his bedroom, the family being wealthy enough in the new China, the economic tiger, to afford such a home for his parents, two sisters, and himself.

He remembered further that that was the day when the official from the party had turned up, saying the younger sister had been arrested in a demonstration in Tiananmen Square and had been taken to a police station but had resisted arrest and had died. He remembered the man had a video that he wants the family to see. The video was of the torture, rape, and murder of his sister. He remembered he hated it; he hated his sister's suffering; he hated the system that did this. He remembered he was only eleven, but he remembered, but most of all his hate was for the uniformed woman who had conducted his sister's murder. He hated the sight of such women; he remembered going to school and seeing uniformed women helping children cross the road, and the hate...

His mind flashed further; he remembered the torture he had taken part in; he remembered the abuse of the victim, even though they were known to be innocent, having just upset a local party official. He then remembered the others; the first he remembered was the night in Hong Kong when he was waiting to meet a contact; he saw a ticket collector in uniform, a Chinese like himself; he felt rage and hatred; he followed the woman until he found himself outside a small office; he heard her on her phone telling a male voice she would be home. Kang remembered how he entered the office and smashed her head against the table until she was dead; he tore at her clothes but did not rape her.

He looked out the window; below in the street, people were living their lives and going to and fro like ants, it seemed, as Kang watched from his tenth-floor office. His mind wandered to the planned escape; he thought about the agreement made the day before with the handler. He was to take a car to the Beijing International Capital Airport, and then once there, he was to make himself known to the airport security that he was there to arrest a British spy. The "spy" was to be taken to the interrogation room and dealt with; during this time, the police with Kang would be replaced by "friendly" police.

Kang would then take the "spy," who would be taken back to the aircraft to point out his accomplice; however, there was no accomplice, and Kang, the police escorts, and the spy were to take their seats, fly to London, and be taken off at the other end. Two Pandas being taken that day to London would be the cover story for the jet's return on the same day when usually it stayed on the ground for two.

Kang thought through the plan, smiled, and guessed the paperwork had already been done; of course, the entire thing had been planned months before. It had been one of three and the best idea. He looked at his watch: 10:30 am, and the plane would be here at 14:45 Beijing time. He would at lunchtime, 1 pm; that should do it. He went back to work dealing with agent reports from the UK.

The time passed quickly. Kang worked well, and just before one, he put the last piece of blank paper in the file, placed it in his safe, and rang down to the carpool and arranged a car, no driver.

Getting the car was, of course, no problem as he drove out towards the airport, he wondered at the real beauty of the plan. The thing was his seniority as a colonel; due to his commitment to the party, his zeal, his job, and of course, the glittering career he had carved, he was, in short, a son of "proven worth," and as such, with his rank, he could buy time if he had to, but more importantly, he could get things done if he needed to.

He drove into the airport, parked the car, and walked towards the entrance for security staff. He went through the sliding door and saw a man, a second-class superintendent, sitting at the desk. He was a plump man, and his plump face gave the colonel a smile. "Can I help you, sir?" The question was answered quickly and promptly. "Yes, I am here to find this man." Kang handed a photo and the flight details he had received from a street food dealer half an hour earlier.

The desk officer looked at the information, picked up his phone, spoke quickly, replaced the receiver, and spoke, "The plane has landed, and the target is aboard, Colonel." "Good, bring him here." Kang was pleased things were going well.

Soon, the spy was brought back, and Kang took him to a room that he had organized. He noticed the man was like himself, in his fifties, tall, and very well-kept. Kang the plan, he started, "Your Mr. Fisher, what is your business here in China?" "I am here to visit Wang Ho Electronics." Fisher's voice did not falter; Kang knew this as a signal and continued, "Please open your case and produce your passport and any other documents." Fisher took everything out on the table, and Kang inspected everything, then came the clincher: "Wang Ho Electronics is in a restricted area. You have no special pass for this."

"I must have forgotten." Fisher played the part well, Kang thought. "I am sorry, Mr. Fisher, you must leave China." "I will escort you to the plane." At that moment, two men entered the room in plain clothes. They told the uniformed officer to go, and as the uniformed officer suspected state security, he was not going to risk his career. He left...

Kang turned to Fisher. "I am going to give you this." Kang handed him a slip of paper explaining in Chinese and English that Mr. Fisher was being deported. These officers and I will escort you. With that, Kang led the way, leading with Fisher behind him and the two agents behind Fisher.

They boarded the bus that was to take them to the plane, the bus empty, apart from this small party and the driver, who, on Kang's arrival, handed an envelope containing boarding passes and British passports for all except Fisher, who had his own anyway. Kang recognized all these actions, and his confidence grew as they approached the aircraft, which. usually stayed on the ground for two days before the next flight. It was now detailed to return to Britain that day with two Pandas and no other passengers; well, at least that was what the Chinese were told.

The group arrived near the plane; the Pandas had been loaded, and now was the critical phase: the party had to board and get sorted in less than ten minutes, as the plane was to take off at four Beijing time; it was now three forty-five. The four men climbed the stairs to the door, and a male flight officer took the passports and boarding cards.

The captain appeared and welcomed the party aboard, saying directly to Kang, "Welcome aboard, Mr. Francis Chong." This broke the silence that was descending. All four men broke into raucous laughter.

CHAPTER 2

The plane took off promptly. The Chinese customs had seen the pandas loaded and safely secured, and as far as they were concerned, that was that. They had not bothered to check the rest, as the customs officer wanted to get home and watch his teenage son play basketball.

The plane was about two hours out of Beijing on what would be a sixteen-hour flight when a woman emerged from the cockpit and introduced herself, Pamela Martin, the vet responsible for the pandas. "I've been upfront," "Bob let me watch take off." Bob, it was ascertained, was the pilot. Kang looked at the short brunette and had an uneasy feeling; he did not like this idea of the vet, but what could he do? She had not been part of the plan, no mention of her, but the pandas did need care, but he felt uneasy. The appearance of anyone was an unexpected problem...

The plane flew on for another hour, then the pilot sent a signal bouncing off a satellite and sending it to a country house in the Chilterns near Buckinghamshire, the house being a safe house for MI6, the SIS Secret Intelligence Service, as it was known. The signal read, "Operation Bird successful; Canary in the cage will bring to pet shop.".

The British, or more specifically the English, have a quaint habit of giving names to their houses; the one where the signal went was called Edgefield, as it was appropriately at the edge of a field. The receiver of the signal was Robert Horton, SIS officer and Kang's contact known as Oliver. He had sent Kang's handler in China to see him when Kang had said he wanted out; Horton had wanted to know why, but

Kang had stayed quiet and refused to tell, only making clear that he, the source of SIS in the Ministry of Security, was at risk.

Now Horton was nearly at the end of the operation; Kang was on his way, and he and Horton had arrangements to confirm: first was bringing Kang to Harvey to meet and then to Edgefield for debriefing, which could take months or years; Kang had been a rich source regarding Chinese actions in the UK. Second was the organization of a new identity and a home and a job, for Kang had to disappear once debriefed.

Horton picked the phone up and rang his boss, Andrew Harvey, head of SIS, "Oliver here; the bird is here soon, ready to give bird seed." Harvey smiled to himself, "Well done; collect when ready and deal with it." Harvey smiled again; Ling Kang was certainly the catch while he was SIS head.

The plane landed on time and was directed to a part of the airport where the pandas were unloaded, and Horton could discreetly meet his guest. The stairs were brought to the plane, and the door opened; first out was the vet, Pamela, who exchanged courtesies with Horton and disappeared toward the Animal Reception Centre at Heathrow to check on the pandas.

Next came the "spy," Fisher; he acknowledged Horton and Horton him. Horton also sent the now-named Alan Richard, the former Fisher, to Edgefield to get debriefed over his part in the escape. The last out were the two policemen and Kang; the policemen were also sent to Edgefield for debriefing. Kang, however, was to come with Horton to meet Harvey, who wanted to see the man behind such a rich source of intelligence.

Horton radioed for the car, which was driven to the plane. Horton opened the back door, and Kang and Horton got in, Horton telling the driver the address where Harvey was and making discreetly sure the driver had a recording of what went on in the car.

Horton began the conversation: "Welcome to the UK! Hope you had a good flight, and I would also like to thank you personally for your help. Kang looked at Horton. He looked at the shorter man, at the blue eyes and the skin that was worn with years of strain. He noticed Horton's hair was turning grey faster than his was; lastly, he noticed how Horton was a man who had not seen a medical test or a gymnasium for years. Kang made his reply using Horton's code name, "Oliver".

"Thank you for the welcome, and considering the risks of the plan, it was easier than expected," Kang had exaggerated the thing, and Horton knew and countered, "Well, everyone played their part." Kang just smiled; Horton followed up, "There was, of course, a risk, but I did not consider with your record and character that thought would work," he quickly added, "My name is Horton, Robert, Colonel Kang," "Kang Ling Colonel, formerly of the Chinese Ministry of State Security, now a traitor." Kang smiled, and Horton could only smile back.

The car pulled up outside their destination, an old Victorian house with steps up to the front door. It had seen better times, and Kang thought it a dark place and not welcoming. Horton got out of the car and ushered Kang to join him. Both men went up the steps, and Horton, when at the front door, rang the doorbell.

The door was opened by Harvey. Kang instantly took him in; he was of average build, a little older than Kang may be, for Kang was 53; Harvey, he guessed, was 56; he found out later that Harvey was 55. He also noticed that Harvey, unlike Horton, had a very different physique, being well-trained and powerfully built; he also suspected that Harvey had seen military service, as he had a bearing of being in control. Something that he had seen with Chinese officers back in Beijing.

"Good evening, gentlemen, so glad you had a safe journey. Would anyone like a drink?" Horton nodded his approval and was handed a whiskey with water and ice. Kang took a coffee from the coffee pot on the table, and Harvey poured himself a whiskey without ice or water, "neat," as he called it. Kang also noted Chinese snacks on the table: baked sweet potato and various seeds and nuts. "Help yourself." Harvey gestured toward the table; the three men helped themselves and then sat down. Harvey struck the first blow. "On behalf of his Majesty's government, may I welcome you to the

United Kingdom, and on behalf of the government, thank you for your service." Kang smiled and said nothing. Harvey followed up with a question: "Why did you ask to defect now?" Kang looked at him and answered with a well-rehearsed lie.

"There was the investigation into the Feng arrest; they were getting close; General Han Cheng began to suspect something.". Harvey thought for a moment and looked at Kang, saying, "Ok, that is understandable; the Feng case did, as we say, upset the applecart." Horton was looking on, and he was thinking about the case. Wan Feng had been a

Chinese secretary at their embassy who had been seeing a civil service executive officer; unfortunately, this man had also been dealing cocaine since university days. The police had got wind of it, raided his flat, and found drugs, the suspect, and Wan Feng in bed with none other than the current Secretary of State for Defence. Life changed for everyone, except Kang, who really had nothing to do with it. However, the Chinese had launched an investigation, and so Kang had to think about running.

CHAPTER 3

Harvey was still pondering the situation. "Well, the Feng case was a problem, and the Chinese were going through everything and may have found you anyway," he finished. "That's enough for tonight."

"We start again tomorrow properly." With that he closed the meeting, sending Horton and Kang to Edgefield, and he went home to his wife and two teenage sons.

Kang sat in the car on the way to Edgefield. He was happy his story had held up; after all, the truth was he had killed a female captain attached to Chéng's office, and unfortunately, she had been Kang's mistress. Kang began to remember how he strangled the officer before tearing at her clothes, leaving her virtually naked. He killed her in the Ministry in Beijing and left the body in a storeroom only for it to be found and Cheng swearing revenge on the killer. Kang had realized he had better get out of China.

"We are nearly there." Horton turned to Kang and smiled, adding further, "This will be home until further notice." "Everything you need will be sent here, and you will not be allowed to leave the house." With those words, the car turned into the driveway, and Edgefield came into view. The house itself was a former vicarage and had been, during the Second World War, an SOE training center. After the war, SIS had turned into a safe house for defectors, and Kang was the next visitor. He could spend weeks or months or even years here as he bared his soul, brain, and heart to his new friends, telling them all about the secrets of his homeland, now so to become a past that Kang had to deal with.

The car pulled up, and a woman came out. Horton caught sight of the gray-haired, slim, and mature lady who, to Kang, looked like a schoolteacher. The woman spoke, "All ready and waiting for food in the dining room." "Good, we will eat and get some rest." Horton made the comment while leading Kang and the lady back into the house.

They entered the house, and Kang looked at his new surroundings. It was exactly as he imagined it would be, as he had seen in pictures of such old houses: the wood paneling, the drawing room, and the dining room, all as he imagined, and now he was no longer managing it.

They arrived in the dining room. "Nice spread, Mrs. Donald. I see we have a theme." "I thought a theme of welcome for the Colonel. "Mrs. Donald acknowledged Kang, who smiled in return and was happy to know the schoolteacher had a name.

Mrs. Donald continued, "I put together spring rolls, various sauces, meatballs, fish, and I thought something English, a chocolate cake." "Very good." Horton motioned for everybody to sit, and soon, the small party of three was enjoying the meal.

At the same moment, in a large townhouse, Andrew Harvey was sitting in his living room with his wife, Anna. He was worried, and his red-haired wife knew it. "What's the matter, darling? "She looked at him directly, giving him the knowing look of something's wrong. What is it? "We have a new guy at work, but he has not settled in well.". Harvey lied to his wife for the umpteenth time because she still thought he worked for the Environment Agency. "Well, what's wrong?" Harvey continued the lie. "We asked him to do a job, but we think he did something else not related, but we can't prove it."

"Well then you have to wait and catch him red-handed."
"Yes," replied Harvey; perhaps it is the only way.

But Harvey did have a real problem. The problem was the reason for Kang defecting; the story of Feng was true, and it was plausible that Kang would have been given the details, as the UK was his area of expertise; there had been an investigation into the case. What had been discovered is that the secretary had been living a double life: a good secretary during the day and a junkie at night. She had not been a spy, and the thing with the Secretary of State had been a complete accident, for he, too had been buying drugs from the civil servant. The investigation led to the recall of the secretary who was shot on her return to Beijing. Kang had not known, and the Chinese had no idea of Kang or his work for SIS. Kang had, therefore lied; the question was whose side was he on? The British Chinese, or American, the last was also plausible that SIS had done the American's work for them; it was not the first time. That was the question of whose side he was on.

The celebration was over, the party had broken up, and Horton had shown Kang his bedroom and asked if he wanted anything else, to which the answer was no. Horton had then wished him good night and left; Kang had sat in the chair thinking about the events of what seemed like the last week but had been nearly only forty-eight hours. He sat, it seemed like forever, but it was a slow thirty minutes. Eventually he tired and went to bed but did not sleep well. At night he would often suffer memories of his sister and the others he had seen and killed. Tonight was such a night. He could not remember his home; his mind drifted back to Hong Kong Airport. July 1995 he was twenty-five years old...

Kai Tak International Airport, Hong Kong, 2nd July 1995.

Captain Ling Kang was waiting in the arrivals hall for his contact; he had been told that his contact was carrying a suitcase with a union jack stamped on it. The contact would put the suitcase down, and Kang would pick it up seconds later and bring it back to the safe house. This was the standard thing that Ling did; it was his job. As a new agent, it was his bread and butter. He saw the contact; the contact put the case down and walked away. Kang slowly walked up to it, picked it up, and walked out of the airport. Then he saw her....

She was a tall blonde with long, flowing hair. She was on her own in the car park where Kang had parked. He noticed her, and he noticed her uniform; he felt himself go cold, and then he felt the rage he usually felt. In such situations, he remembered the Chinese female officer standing in the corner of the room in which his sister was being tortured, the officer shouting at her and encouraging the three policemen as they assaulted, beat, and took turns in raping her orally, anally, and vaginally.

Kang noticed the air hostess, for that is what she was, standing by a car and looking for the car keys. She opened the door. Kang saw her bend over, and with his rage exploding through him like a volcanic explosion, he ran toward the woman, pushed her from behind, and with both hands grabbed her round the throat and began to strangle her, the grip tightening every time a wave of rage went through him, hitting his soul and heart like waves hitting the shore. Soon, he felt the body go limp. He felt his rage still; he began tearing at her clothes until every article was out of place and she was virtually naked. By now his rage had subsided. And he looked at the body, a calmness now over him; he returned to his car, climbed in, and drove to the safe house.

CHAPTER 4

The body was found by the victim's friend, who called the police. The first on the scene was a Land Rover full of constables, both British and Chinese. They sealed off the scene of the crime and waited for the support that would undoubtedly come.

Soon, the support arrived, the most important being Detective Chief Inspector George Davies, aged forty-three and of a wiry stature; the 5'8 man was of slim build, with a dark blonde mop of hair that looked unkempt even though he combed it regularly. He found the senior constable. "Alright, who was she?" "Her name was Christine Edwards, twenty-four years old and an air hostess with Singapore Airlines. "The constable had taken notes, and Davies was pleased that it was a good start; usually, these things were not. "Who found her?" Davies looked at the Black woman who had been crying. Davies found out her name: Cynthia Jones.

"I'm Detective Chief Inspector George Davies, "he went on. I am so sorry you had to find the body. How well did you know Christine Edwards?" " She was a friend. We were on the same flight today, which is rare. We were going to have supper in the hotel and swim later," Cynthia began to cry, big teardrops running down her face, reflected by the summer Hong Kong sun.

While Davies was interviewing Cynthia, the pathologist turned up, conducted a quick examination, and walked up to Davies, who told Cynthia that was enough for today, but, if necessary, she would need to be where she could question again if any new leads occurred. Cynthia told him they were, at that moment, sharing a hotel room.

"Well, what can you tell me?" Davies paid attention to the skinny, tall woman in front of him who went by the name Dr. Amanda Redman. "Strangled but not raped, clothes torn off, but no sexual assault. Rigor mortis has not completely set in; she has been dead about three hours." Davies looked at his watch; it said three o'clock, so midday was the killing or thereabouts.

Davies saw the undertakers arrive. He knew they would take the body back to the pathologist lab for a full examination. The detective turned to the pathologist: Let me know the results of your autopsy, please, as soon as possible. This last piece of information annoyed Dr. Redman, who retorted, "I will take as long as necessary; autopsies are not easy. "Try your best," with that turned away and headed back to the office. Back at the office he saw his detective sergeant, Robert Evans, a big Welsh rugby player when not a policeman. Davies brought him up to date and sent him off to check the hotel room and see if he could get more from Cynthia Jones, for his first thought was the victim knew the killer.

THE PRESENT

Kang lay still; he was feeling tired. The thoughts going through his head had felt painful, each one recreating a past he did not want to live with and reawakening a hatred that he despised but could not control because he had the female officer in his mind in the room with his sister. He often wondered why he was like this, not really understanding the rage completely, but only knowing a woman in uniform brought on a rage that he had to release. He began to feel tired, and soon morphia had eventually won.

The dawn broke over the New Forest in Hampshire, England, but the sun did not shine through because of the heavy mist that covered the landscape near the village of Lyndhurst. Just outside the village, there was a lonely cottage with one inhabitant, former Detective Chief Inspector George Davies. Davies had left Hong Kong just before the handover and had taken a job with the Thames Valley Police, being a detective based as Kidlington, the HQ of Thames Valley Police. He had retired at fifty-five in two thousand and seven and bought his cottage in Hampshire and was living the life of a contented but lonely man, as his wife Sarah, who was Chinese, had died unexpectedly of a heart attack just after Alpha File had been laid to rest in strange circumstances. He had left Hong Kong alone and had been alone ever since.

His mind drifted back to the Alpha File, the serial killer also given the name Alpha. It often happened because the entire thing had been his biggest failure, or the biggest cover-up, for the intervention of Hong Kong's Special Branch, those police that dealt with political things and national security. His mind drifted back to the second killing, one of their own, a policewoman. ....

Hutchison Park, Hong Kong, 30ᵗʰ July 1995

"Who was she?" "Constable Sandra Wu, age 26, has been in the police for three years." Davies and his sergeant Evans were looking at the dead and naked body of the policewoman. Davies went on, "Who found her?" "A park gardener," replied Evans. "I questioned him, and all he could tell me was he found her here with her clothes strewn around her." "Alright, we will wait for the pathologist." Davies was thinking quickly: two identical killings exactly four weeks apart must be a serial killer, perhaps?

While pondering this, Dr. Redman turned up; she examined the body while Davies watched. She turned to the detective. "Just like the first one, the air hostess, strangled, stripped, but no sexual assault. Looks like we got our hands full." "Anything from the first one?" Davies asked the question in the hope he would have the vital clue, but nothing, out of Dr. Redman's mouth except, "No, just like the last one." She went on, "I've just had a thought: you remember the ticket collector at the railway station?" "Yes. "Davies suddenly became attentive. Redman continued, "Well, that victim was like the air hostess and the victim now." "But she had her head smashed in." Davies could not make the connection. Redman saw his problem: "Yes, I know different methods, but the same stripped but not assaulted or raped; it is the same killer. "Alright, Dr., we will assume one killer." Davies was still not too sure, but he would go with the theory. In the meantime, he sent Evans to tell Officer Wu's parents and check her flat. Also, now three killings if Redman was right.

The Present

As Davies came out of his reminiscing, he was in the small office he had created so he could pay bills and keep his old files in order, among which, when he had retired, he had copies of the Alpha File made. His mind returned to Hong Kong, six unsolved murders, and the intervention of the state, for reasons unknown, or more precisely, in defense of the Hong Kong and British state, the reasons this was not Davies's concern, of course, he just had to follow orders from those above him.

While Davies was thinking about the Alpha File, Colonel Lin Kang had been in his debriefing session for two hours; his interviewers were Horton and Harvey. They had started off with his recruitment at the end of British rule in Hong Kong; hours before the handover, Kang had walked into the governor's mansion and made it known he wanted to help the British and to prove the point he had brought a list of Chinese agents in Britain.

At first no one had believed him, and eventually, after some discussion and confirmation of Kang's identity and checking a couple of names on the list, Kang was sent away with instructions to contact them when the British were ready and not to do anything until then.

Horton and Harvey were looking at Kang. "Well, that was the beginning of our relationship." Horton's words filled the room as he looked at his papers, making sure his questions were in order and Kang would answer as Horton wanted. Harvey continued: Ok, we'll talk about your work for us in China, and then we'll finish for the day. So, they spent the next eight hours, including lunch, discussing and questioning Kang over his activities on behalf of the SIS in China; they talked about the agents Kang had blown in the UK and the operations he had wrecked, also in the UK. They talked about China things files. Kangg had passed information on the structure of the ministry and, most importantly, the important people who were at the top of the ministry. Kang had betrayed the lot.

In Britain the time was 10 am, in Beijing it was 6 pm, and General Han Cheng was explaining the disappearance of Colonel Lin Kang. He was talking to Ji Wu, a Politburo member tasked with conducting the interview. "So you don't really know what happened to Kang." Wu's impatience was obvious. "No, we don't know exactly," Cheng answered with what was a half-lie; he had a good idea what happened but dared not admit it yet. Wu was in no mood. "It has been three days, and you have nothing. Let me tell you, I have it on good authority from my own source that Colonel Kang has been working for and now defected to the British." Cheng looked astonished. How had this man known, and what source? "Your source is good, and of course we will work hard to deal with the traitor." Cheng had to regain some ground for guessing his job and maybe his life was on the line.

Wu remained unimpressed. "You will operate against the traitor and find out what has been betrayed and how we can deal with it. I will, of course, be following events". Cheng thought for a moment, "Can I use your source "? "Only through me." Wu was not going to lose his source, for it was his private connection from when he had been a state security official. "Now General Cheng gets to work because the traitor, we believe has been working for years." With that, Wu left, shutting the door loudly behind him.

CHAPTER 5

Wu had finished with Cheng at approximately 8 pm Beijing time. In Britain, it was 12 pm. Kang was having lunch in the dining room with Mrs. Donald; Horton and Harvey had left for a local hotel, which was usually used when things of a serious nature like now. They were just finishing when Harvey opened the conversation: "Nice bit of beef; do you believe Kang? "Horton thought for a moment and then said, "Well, it is difficult; we have no real answer to why he wanted to defect. The Feng story was unlikely, as we know, but there is something else." "Well, how do we find out? "Harvey was not too sure where this was going; Horton enlightened him. "You remember the Sokolov affair, the Russian we thought was a defector but was a plant. Remember how we caught him?" Harvey remembered they had suspicions about Ivan Sokolov, so they had set a trap. A press conference was called, and Sokolov was put before the cameras; at the same time, a watch was put on a house that Sokolov was living in, and sure enough, Sokolov had contacted a member of the Soviet embassy. The idea was that if Sokolov was a double agent, he would need to tell his controller all was well, and it was thought a TV press conference would flush out Sokolov, as his controller could see the British had taken the bait. Then a contact would need to see Sokolov, and they would have him. Harvey remembered they SIS had let this happen once more, and the third time, they had trapped him. Afterwards Sokolov had been swapped for an agent working for the British. Harvey looked at Horton. "Do you think it would work again?" "Why not?" Horton seemed confident. He continued, I don't think Kang would suspect anything;

besides, we could always use Jimmy and Roger; they could keep an eye on him." Harvey seemed to think that was a good idea. "Yes, I will get them here. By the way, do you know where they are by any chance? I will have to dig them out from wherever." Horton said, "There at 'The Bridges'". "The Bridges" was the training center for "tough guys," those whose job was to protect and sometimes not those who threatened the British State. "I get Simpson, the course leader, to send them here as soon as possible." Horton knew Simpson would be there, and both men would be at Edgefield by tonight.

Sure enough, Jimmy and Roger turned up that evening, and Horton took them into the dining room to see their new charge. Kang was sitting at the table reading a document Horton had shown him about the infiltration of Chinese students in British universities. "Lin, I want you to meet your new careers; they will be looking after you while you're here." Kang looked at the two men; the first one, Jimmy, was what later Kang described "as a short, fat, Black man," and Roger was "a skinny, white guy." He could add Jimmy needed to see a gym desperately and Roger's teeth a dentist. Horton interrupted Kang's thoughts. "From now on, I or someone else will come and see you when we need to. Jimmy and Roger have been tasked with all your needs; they will, from now on, see to everything." With that, Horton said his goodbyes turned around and left Kang with the "babysitters.".

Outside, Horton found his phone rang Harvey. "Have the babysitters in place and have told the babysitters what is needed." "Good, "said Harvey. "Now I will arrange part two and let you know when ready.". Horton acknowledged

Harvey and then put his phone away. Soon, we would know about Colonel Lin Kang, he thought to himself.

Harvey, at the other end, after dealing with Horton, turned to the short, rotund woman sitting opposite him in his office. "Right, Anna, you heard the conversation, and I told you what we want. When do you think you can do it?" Anna Yates looked directly at Harvey through the mop of blonde hair that always seemed unkempt and uncut despite her best efforts at hair care.

"Should be easy enough," Anna replied. "We can run the interview and put the program out within forty-eight hours." "Ok, good, then I will go tomorrow and organize the interview and check up on our star." Anna smiled at the thought of a news headline for her TV company and the kudos for her. As for Harvey, he was also pleased with the story he had concocted and caught Anna, and the real reason for the interview was a well-kept secret.

While all this was going on, Kang had been getting to know his "babysitters," Jimmy and Roger. Jimmy was of Nigerian descent and had arrived in Horton's employment by way of the royal marines and an accidental meeting when Jimmy was on a fitness course at "The Bridges." Horton had seen potential in Jimmy and had recruited him as a personal aid. Same with Roger, though Horton had found him as down and out in London. He, Roger, had been a paratrooper, and after service, he had fallen on hard times, only to be found by Horton, who had wanted contact about Irish terrorism, and Roger knew all the connections, both good and bad, in North London, as by now he was a petty criminal.

Kang and the babysitters had been playing cards and had been talking about their military experiences. Jimmy had been telling about his family in Britain and Nigeria as Kang had been to Africa once soon after joining the ministry. He had been on a scouting mission looking for low-level contacts. Afterward, Kang had gone to bed and had tried to sleep but could not; he had remembered the Hong Kong policewomen he had killed.

HUTCHISON PARK, HONG KONG, 30TH JULY 1995

Kang had just picked up his "post" from the letterbox that had been created in the park. The letterbox was in fact, under the bandstand in the center of the park; the drop-off point was just under the small staircase that led up to the platform.

Kang was on his way back home when he heard a commotion; he saw two police officers chase a pickpocket into the area of the park where he was. He saw them separate, and he saw the female officer head off in another direction to cut the pickpocket off. Kang knew it was a pickpocket because in the noise someone had shouted, "Pickpocket!". He saw the female officer and her uniform, and his blind rage suddenly came upon him, and he followed the officer to a small coppice; there he had grabbed her, and with his bare hands, he had strangled her, crushing her Adam's apple, and then savagely tearing at her clothes, clawing and pulling and tearing until she was naked. Then he felt the anger subside, and he knelt over her and wept until he heard a voice and fled.

THE PRESENT

Kang had woken up from his nightmare or bad memory; he himself could never be sure of what it really was or how it came about. He only knew that they happened when they did; he would see flashes in his mind from the past, and that would set him off on his emotional roller coaster that always appeared when least expected. He sat up in bed and began to think about his situation, the debriefing, which still had a long way to go. Horton and Harvey were a straightforward case, both officers like himself and professional, Jimmy and Roger, and Mrs. Donald were cogs in the wheel.

Kang thought about how long he would be here, in Edgefield, probably years, he thought, as he had much to tell. Kang thought about China and what was happening there. He expected, of course, that General Cheng would ask him to find him if Cheng was, of course, alive and not shot for his stupidity in not seeing Kang's defection. He thought about how they may track him down and wondered whose side his new friends were really on and who their contacts were; no doubt there would be a Beijing agent among them ordered to look for the Traitor Colonel Lin Kang. It may be difficult times ahead.

CHAPTER 6

Kang had finally slept at midnight in Beijing; it was 8 am, and Ji Wu was in his office in the Zhongnanhai compound, which houses the communist party and China's government. He was sitting at his desk drinking Western coffee and smoking Western cigarettes when his phone rang. He picked up the receiver and heard his contact from the foreign ministry, "Kang is in Britain; he got out by an aircraft carrying two pandas to Britain; a supporter in London told us the news. He got it from a contact who is a sympathizer, who was on the same flight looking after the pandas". Wu was ecstatic; what a piece of luck! The first real break and Cheng was still struggling to find out the basics. In fact, he wondered why this was; it was because Cheng was a loyal party member and largely did as he was told, and that meant he was investigating Kang's background and his work, and he was probably dealing with espionage, whereas he, Wu, wanted the man, and now he was going to get him. He replied to his caller, "Can you find out more and let me know?" "Of course came the reply." Wu put the phone down, satisfied. Minutes later the phone rang; it was Cheng. "I have started the investigation to see what he has betrayed; it seems we have lost at least ten years work to him, including the dragon chain." "Very well, keep me informed and find him." Wu put the phone down and knew he was right about Cheng doing everything to order. As for the Dragon Chain, it was disappointing as it was a source of good espionage for software material; the Oxford and Bath groups were useful but not that important. What was important was the fact that

Kang may have found the rings that he, Wu, was still running. Wu then went back to work happy.

2 PM THE KING'S ARMS, A PUBLIC HOUSE IN LONDON

The short brunette was sitting at a table waiting for her appointment. Ever since she had told him about her flight from Beijing with the Pandas and four other unexpected people, the guest who was coming to see her had shown a great interest in the Chinaman she described. Pamela Martin, however, was worried. She was sympathetic to communism and had found herself in the Mao camp after the fall of the Soviet Union. She looked towards the entrance, her brown eyes looking nervous as the man she was meeting was a diehard communist with absolute belief in "historic materialism.".

Pamela Martin began to think about herself and what she had done and what to say now. She had been a communist sympathizer since university, having been born into a middle-class family, and she had, of course, turned against her parents after a trip to Africa, and she had seen the poverty and had clashed with a Western businessman who made it clear that the Africans did not matter when it came to profit-making. She also thought about the situation now; if she had not opened her mouth, she would not have been told to come today and tell the full story. Now, what to say? Well, she thought the truth was all.

She was still in deep thought when Chris Edward came through the door and caught her eye; they both smiled, and she noticed that the glasses-wearing Chris was carrying a file.

He was also dressed in his usual fashion: jeans, a shirt, and a jacket with his blue glasses and the short back and sides hairstyle that he always wore for his jet-black hair. "What are you drinking?" He noticed the empty glass. "Red wine," Pamela said. "Ok, so wine and a beer." Chris went to get the drinks, and Pamela settled herself down. Chris returned, "Here's your wine." He smiled again and, sat down and continued, "Take a look at this first.". Chris opened the file and took out a picture of a man in his early fifties with greying hair and features that could be said to be hawk-like: his pointed nose, the set eyes, the mouth that, when closed seemed to hold everything. "Is this the man?" Pamela looked and thought and looked at Chris, "That's him, the one on the aircraft." Pamela put her wine down, and Chris went on, "Tell me exactly again what you saw." Pamela started to think again and remembered first at a party when she had told Chris about the encounter when he had mentioned that someone had betrayed his beloved communist way of life.

Chris pushed her on: "Tell me." By now, there was a menace in his voice. Pamela replied, "Well, I was with the pilot, and he allowed me to sit in the cockpit, and then I went to see the pandas, and that's when I saw this man." "Did he give a name?" "No," said Pamela, "but he is the man in the photograph." "Alright," Chris looked content. "I won't need you again." Pamela felt relief; her mind went back to the party when Chris had mentioned this man, and she had said she had a funny experience...

About an hour later, Chris was walking home from a Chinese restaurant, having delivered a message to the owner, who would, in due course, pass the message on to a diplomat at the Chinese embassy. Chris got to his front door, and as he was unlocking it, his phone rang. He looked at the screen; the number he saw was one he knew was only to be used as an emergency contact. He accepted the call. A female Asian voice came on. "Thank you for your help, but we may need you again. We have found out that the traitor is in Britain, but we need more help." "Ok, do I need to do more now?" "No, but that will change." Chris thought for a second, acknowledged the voice, and turned the phone off.

The voice that Edward had spoken to belonged to Captain Zhi Liu, Ministry of State Security. She was sitting in the living room of the bungalow rented in the village of Barsett just outside of London. She had been tasked with contacting Chris Edward by her controller, who she knew only as "Shizi" or "lion" in English. Now, she had to report the conversation and take instructions if any were to be given. She next moved rooms from the living room to the workroom that was meant for painting, as being an artist as her cover, she being what is called an "illegal," meaning she was in Britain illegally under a false name, or rather a name taken from someone dead but brought back to life as the spy, her personal history, showed this. Her cover was, in fact, one Jenny Ling, a Hong Kong woman who had died in San Francisco; the body and documents had been found by a Chinese agent in the San Francisco Police Department, the details being passed to Beijing, who "washed," or prepared a story or "legend" based on the information given, and created the "legend" or story of Jenny Ling as Zhi Liu was known to her friends and locals in the village.

Liu opened her laptop and went to the chat room that "Lion" had created. She had never met Lion but had been approached by someone from the Zhongnanhai, the communist party headquarters, and told that she was to do important work. Zhi Liu looked at the screen and saw Lion was already there. Liu read the first message. "Good evening, Jenny, have you spoken to Sparrow?" Sparrow, being Chris Edward, messaged back, "Yes," and asked for further instructions. Lion sent back that there were no further instructions, as "Robin" had the situation in hand. Liu had no idea who Robin was, but it did not matter; she was not to know in any case. She acknowledged Lion, and with that, she shut down the laptop and went to make an early supper.

All this had taken place between 4 to 4:30 pm in Britain; in Beijing, it was 12:30 am, and Ji Wu was sitting at his desk, feeling satisfied that he had the situation under control. Cheng, by contrast, had gotten himself into a real mess when the body of his mistress had been found, and Cheng was himself under real suspicion as a traitor. His investigation had come to a halt. Wu also thought about his contact in the foreign ministry who had told him in the first place. It was lucky this contact and "Robin" had been old friends that Wu was glad the friendship was still alive; useful fool, he thought. After all, Robin had told his friend he needed help, as he, Robin, had panicked when Kang had appeared.

CHAPTER 7

"Well, that's the plan, Lin." Horton had spent the morning talking to Kang and talking about the interview that Kang would give about his defection. Kang had asked why this was planned as it was; Horton had said that it was thought important that people had to be shown what the Beijing regime was and how it acted. Kang agreed and asked when the interview would take place. Horton told him in two days' time. Kang was satisfied.

After talking to Kang, Horton had spoken to Harvey; Harvey had asked if Kang suspected anything. Horton said no; Kang suspected nothing. Harvey was satisfied Horton had asked what the security arrangements were; Harvey had told just the usual: Kangs's voice was to be disguised, and his face was to be blacked out. Horton asked about getting into the studio; Harvey confirmed the back entrance through the basement of the TV HQ. Horton was glad, so then Harvey said his goodbyes and told Horton to look after Kang, and they would speak after the interview.

At about the same time as Horton and Harvey were talking, Ben Davey was in a pub getting slowly drunk. He was, by trade or profession, a freelance photographer or, more simply, a paparazzi, a term he did not like. He also did not like the fact he was down on his luck and had no job. He was contemplating his position when he suddenly remembered a story he had been told by an American journalist who got it from a Japanese person working in Beijing who got it from a Japanese embassy official. Ben thought for a moment he was down on his luck since the pandemic; things had been tough, and freelancing was getting tougher. He thought further; he began to remember the story: The Chinese had found the body of a secretary at the Ministry of State Security, and at the same time, the head of the British section had disappeared; defected, the claim was to Britain. Ben thought further, thinking it was a stupid idea, but then again perhaps it was a chance; the question was now where to start...

Anna Yates was at her desk when her phone rang. "Hello, Anna Yates, editor," she announced in the clipped professional tones she used on the phone. "Anna, it's Ben Davey." "Ben, she smiled, it's been a long time. What are you doing now?" "Still freelancing, but times are hard," Ben answered in a matter-of-fact voice. "Sorry to hear that," Anna smiled as she thought of the good times she had had with Ben and his friends when she was a newspaper reporter. Ben made his pitch. "I have heard that we have a Chinese defector in Britain, and I remembered you dealt with the Russian." "That was years ago, and we have no Chinese defectors to talk to, just a Chinese man for an article on living in Britain.". "You don't think he is one and the same?" Davey pressed home. "No, he is not. He has been living here for years." Ben paused for a second; he guessed Anna was either not telling the truth, and she did know, or she was herself on the trail of the interviewee (which she was not). "Ok, Anna, by the way, when is this interview to take place?" "Day after tomorrow," came the reply, "alright, perhaps I get a picture." "Maybe there is a rumour he is coming through the back entrance; security has been alerted." "I see. Ok, well, I'll see you sometime." "Ok." With that, Ben Davey put the phone down. He was getting a sudden interest in immigrant life, and he knew the back entrance was on Westgate Road.

Two days later, Davey was waiting for his victim. He had no idea of the time; however, he knew the interview was live, and the program would be going out at seven in the evening; therefore, the target would arrive at five to get ready in the makeup room, and that meant he would have to be here at four fifty. He also thought about the photo itself and decided that as Westgate Road was a one-way system, he would take the photo from his car parked in the convenient car park right opposite the studio's back entrance. He had the plan worked out: take the shot and dive out of sight. He had done it before.

"We will be there in ten minutes, and through the back entrance, nice and quiet, no need for a major operation, you understand," Horton looked at Kang sitting in the back seat of the car with Roger while Jimmy drove. "Roger will go with you when you leave the car.". With that, Horton sat back and waited for them to arrive.

The car pulled as Ben expected; he was watching from his car camera at the ready. The passenger door on the curbside opened, and a man got out. He was short, his hair was greying, and he looked overweight; his name was Horton, but Ben had no idea. Then the rear passenger opened, and a skinny guy got out with a Chinaman, the fittest looking one of the lot. Davey began to take pictures, the camera clicking quickly as Kang swung around slightly, and the camera caught his face straight on. On that one, Davey stopped and dived into the well seat of his car.

"Right off you go, Kang Jimmy, and I will stay close by and come back around seven fifteen and then home. Hope it goes well. See you later". With that, Horton got into the car, said something inaudible to Jimmy, and then they were gone.

Ben was watching while this was going on. He waited while the street cleared. Then he started his car and drove home to develop the pictures and then find a buyer, and he had a good idea who.

"How did it go?" Horton had a big smile on his face as Kang emerged from the studios; he was happy to see the Chinaman again, as the thought of him being killed was a nightmare. "It went well." Kang returned the smile, but he was not too happy. When getting out of the car, he saw something—or thought he did—and he was quite sure someone was there but was not sure if the other three had seen it. But he was sure there was something there.

Later at Edgefield all was quiet; supper had been eaten, and Kang had had his private time. Now, it was a bed for another day of debriefing. But Kang could not rest; the idea that he was being watched did not leave, and at the same time, he began to remember another sunny day and a video camera...

Conrad Pacific Hotel, 88 Queensway, Admiralty, Hong Kong, 4th August 1995.

Kang was sitting on the bed. He was looking at the lifeless body at his feet, naked and with a grotesque look on her face. When Kang had strangled her, she had been a chambermaid in the hotel, but no more, not ever. His mind drifted back over the last hour: first meeting his contact, being given the package, then seeing the contact go and waiting to leave so no one would connect the two. But in waiting, a chambermaid had come in. Kang had allowed her in and had watched her. He remembered, remembered watching and the feeling of pain in his heart and the sickness of his stomach as he remembered his sister...

He struck out and grabbed the woman around the throat and began to tighten his grip, and soon the woman began to fade; her violent kicking slowly subsided as the life flowed out to be replaced by a cold, unrelenting flow of death entering. Kang then, now in his frenzy, tore at the clothes until she was naked, and then his hate subsided. He was alone again. He quickly picked up the package and left; he was still in a daze, not realizing what was going on. He entered the lift and pressed the button to the ground floor; then he noticed the camera...

CHAPTER 8

"Who's the victim? "Detective Chief Inspector George Davies had just arrived, his sergeant and Dr. Amanda Redman, "Number four now, just like all the rest. " Dr. Redman interrupted just as Evans was about to answer Davis's question. Davis retorted, "I know, and still no real leads." Evans eventually chipped in, "Sarah Li, 23 years old, studying medicine but being a chambermaid as a part-time job." "Who found her?" "A guest. She was pretty cut up; I still got to talk to her." Evans looked at his boss; he then brightened up, "We have a picture. He was caught on camera in the lift." Davis smiled. "Good, let's get a copy and put it out as a public announcement and see what happens." "In the meantime, let me have a look." Evans handed him a still. Davis looked at it. He studied carefully; he saw a young man with features that could be said to be hawk-like: his pointed nose, the set eyes, the mouth that was full-lipped, and long fingers attached to thin hands. But the one thing the detective noticed was the eyes; they were haunted, fearful, staring. They were the eyes of a frightened and probably very disturbed individual.

Davies also interviewed the hotel guest who had found the body, Mrs. Angela Erickson, who had newly arrived in the colony to join her husband, a banker. She really did not have much to say; she just told the detective that she had collected the key from reception and she was staying for a week while her husband was moving stuff into their new home in the New Territories. She went up to the fifth floor and found her room, opened the door, and ....

Davies told Mrs. Erickson that she had been helpful, and if needed again, she would be called on, but Davies knew full well that would not be the case.

He also had the photograph circulated, and plenty of witnesses came forward, and soon, Davis had several sightings of his suspect. He also, unfortunately had Special Branch on his back.

Special Branch appeared in his office three days after the photo had been made public; its appearance was in the shape of Chief Superintendent David Low, and he was in no mood to discuss or compromise; no prisoners were to be taken. "D.I. Davies, I ask you to surrender everything you have on Alpha and the Alpha file. "No matter, those files are to be handed over." Low was being insistent, and the situation made worse when Detective Chief Inspector Paul Rodman, Davies's immediate chief, entered the room, looked at the two men, and just said, "George, hand it all over; there is nothing we can do." Davies was crestfallen; slowly, he went to the filing cabinet, took out the Alpha File, and laid it on the desk. Low picked it up, glanced through it, and left the room. Davies looked at his chief. "There must be something we can do." "No, nothing." Rodman looked at his subordinate, saying, "These orders came from the top of the tree.".

The Office of Greg Walker, Editor of the Messenger Newspaper

Greg Walker was sitting at his desk; he was reading the latest copy of the "Messenger." Two days before, he had spoken to Ben Davey, a freelance photographer who had sold him a story of a Chinese defector supported by several good photographs. At first Walker had thought it was a bad idea, but as he had no good story for his newspaper now, he went with it. Now, he was having real doubts.

It had started the day before the photos had been published, and within three hours at lunchtime, his phone had rung, and a man called "Allanson" had spoken to him, telling him that the photo was to be withdrawn and the files from where the photo came to be handed over to a member of Special Branch, which was duly done that mid-afternoon. Walker had rung his lawyer, but someone had got to them, they telling Walker he could forget freedom of the press. Walker realized whatever it was or whoever it was, the photo had upset a lot of people.

"Allanson" AKA Robert Horton, had felt satisfied he had dealt with the editor, and reporting to Harvey, he made it clear that everything was ok and the damage limited, so anyone who had seen the photo did not have much clue as to where to start looking for Kang; of course, if they did, then SIS, MI5, and Special Branch had the chance of dealing with it quickly, as Kang was high on the secure list. However, two people had seen the photo and had a great interest in the Chinese man; one was a former policeman, and the other a Chinese agent.

George Davies had been in his local newsagent when he happened to see the photo; for a second, he did not recognize the man, but then suddenly, he remembered the still photo from the lift in the Conrad Pacific Hotel, 88 Queensway, Admiralty, Hong Kong, 4th August 1995. He went home, found the photo, compared it with a copy of the messenger, and realized that the "defector" may be the Hong Kong serial killer he had searched for so long. The question was what to do. He felt he had to do something; after all, he promised the parents of Sandra Wu and Sarah Li that he would catch their daughter's killer. But he had not; Hong Kong was returned to China, and Davies had been sent home to serve and finally retire. Now, he was sitting in his living room, a tired and lonely widower. George Davies had no real idea what to do. He just did not know, then it came suddenly; he got his wind-up, and he would try and make things right, if not for the victims or their families, at least for himself. But where to start? He sat and thought; then he remembered Peter Roy; he was something in the Special Branch in Hong Kong, and he had a connection with the Davies murder squad. The problem was he had been paralyzed in an accident and was now, as George saw it, "confined to a wheelchair." He remembered though Peter did not see it like that; indeed, since his accident, he had become quite a political animal. Davies had one telephone number; perhaps Peter was still connected to it. Davies decided to try.

The second person to see the photo was Captain Zhi Liu, or Jenny Ling, as she was known to her village inhabitants. She, too, had seen the photo in a newsagent, but unlike George Davies, she knew exactly who it was and what to do about it. She went home, started up her laptop, entered the chat room, and left a message for "Lion." The message was simple. Kang was indeed in the UK, and she needed instructions on how to proceed and any further instructions about her own work on student recruitment at the art college she was working at, having recently applied for and gained the role of tutor to her afternoon group.

It was 8 pm in Beijing when Ji Wu read the message from Jenny. He already knew that "Robin" had thought Kang was in Britain when two of his best men were taken away from him. Now Jenny had confirmed it. Now to deal with the traitor, but how? He thought about his options. First, he could discredit the traitor by creating a story to seed doubt in the mind of SIS. But how to do that is some kind of trick. He thought the best way was probably to create a legend for SIS to chase. The second option was to kill Kang, and here it was obvious Robin would be the assassing. And he was ultimately expendable as his only activity was to report on the security SIS used. As for getting Robin to cooperate, he could promise exile in China, even though it was a lie; Robin would believe it. Also, the added advantage was that Robin could be blamed as a lunatic, and China was free of suspicion. He would have to consider the entire thing.

Peter Roy picked up the phone within seconds of it ringing. He heard an unfamiliar voice. "Is this Peter Roy's address, George Davies, former Hong Kong police?" Davies played it straight in case it was a wrong address. "Yes, I remember. "Nice to hear from our." Peter had only just remembered the former policeman, as the name was not immediately familiar. Davies was relieved; he continued, "I come straight to the point: you remember the serial killings in 1995? Your lot halted my investigations; now I found him again, and I want him brought to justice." "How can I help?" Peter started to sound cautious. Davis went on. "Yes, Special Branch stopped my investigation. I want to know why. "I don't know why," Roy responded with a plea. "Well, you were in my office at the time." Davies pressed home hard, waiting for a response. "I really can't help you; I didn't have the security clearance." Davies jumped at the chance. "But you were in my office when your chief, David Low, ended my involvement." Roy listened and thought after what seemed like hours, even though it was minutes, finally saying, "Alright, can you visit tomorrow?" We do need to talk about Alpha, The Alpha." Davies was astonished that Roy knew the name of his investigation.

CHAPTER 9

They met at Roy's home two days after the telephone call. Davies arrived and was now sitting in Peters's living room. Roy had offered him a drink, and Davies accepted a whiskey. Roy moved his wheelchair to the other side of the table, looked at Davies, and began, "Alright, what do you want from me?" "First, how did you know about the file and the suspect code name? Secondly, why was it stopped?" Davies asked the first of what he saw as many important questions.

Roy looked at him and paused; he looked thoughtful. He then looked directly at the former detective and said, "To answer the second question, Kang had walked into the governor's mansion and made it known he wanted to help the British; he had with him a list of Chinese agents. We did not believe him to begin with, but we checked Kang's out and his names list, and then we put him on ice until we were ready to work him." Roy continued, "You were stopped because of Kang's value to us; he was too important. We suspected he was your killer, but his importance to us meant that he could not be apprehended. There were also the problems if you made an arrest; arresting a Chinese spy for murder would have been a problem, especially as his activity, aside from his spying, would have caused an almighty row."

Roy waited for a response, but there was none, so he finished his lecture: "We knew the name of the file and the codename of the suspect because I went through your file on a need-to-know basis; your former boss, Detective Chief Inspector Paul Rodman, let us read everything only he and we knew.

Davies looked astonished at the lies and deceit; he felt he should not have been surprised, but he was still shocked at his boss's betrayal, as he had a lot of respect for Rodman. Roy noticed he followed up. "You should not be naive; you should know how we work. "And for your information, Kang is here in the UK, and the SIS doesn't know about his extracurricular activities. We decided, on balance, as I have already explained, that it was more important he was a spy for us.".

Davies eventually regained his voice. "So, you as Special Branch and us as the police knew about his killings," "and SIS did not." Davies stared at the former Special Branch man, sitting in his wheelchair with a well-built upper body gained through months of rehab and no doubt a desire to survive and achieve his objective. But he did not feel sorry for the man; he still felt angry at the treachery.

Roy could read Davies's face, "I know you don't think much of me, but we were operating and working in an international environment that meant the stakes were high, higher than dealing with a serial killer. "Davies said nothing apart from, "I think I better go." With that, Davies got up and left. Roy left a parting shot: "By the way, there is no more Special Branch; it is now Counter Terrorism Command."

As Davies drove home, he was angry and upset. Angry at what had happened and upset at the fact he had not found out where Kang was. He wanted to bring Kang to justice but had not found where he was; he only knew why things had turned out as they did. Davies was going to have to think again.

At the same moment, Peter Roy had been on WhatsApp, sending an alert to Chief Superintendent Allan Roberts. In his message, he told the superintendent that if anyone asked for or about Alpha, he was to contact this WhatsApp number belonging to a senior counterterrorism officer. So, he contacted me. Superintendent Allan Roberts listened to his story and assured him all would be taken in hand, and an alpha would be dealt with.

He was true to his word; later that evening, he arranged for me to meet the cabinet secretary, Sarah Lewis. The meeting would take place at the RAF Museum Hendon in Hangars 3 and 4 amongst the Spitfires and Messerschmitts of 1940 fame.

Sarah Lewis was of medium build in her late forties, dressed for business in a blue jacket and skirt, her red hair flowing to shoulder length; her hair highlighted her green eyes. Roberts was wearing a black suit and tie; it complemented the blonde and blue-eyed policeman, who, being over six feet tall, was a valuable player in one of the lock positions on his local rugby team. Sarah Lewis kicked off the conversation: "Well, this is a nasty shock. I thought we had a policy agreed." "We did, and we still do." Roberts rankled at the woman's attitude; after all, it was only a retired policeman not willing to let go of a past case. Sarah Lewis struck hard. "Well, when your people discovered what Colonel Kang was doing, you should have told SIS." Roberts looked at her. "In 1996, Chief Superintendent David Low, of our department when it was Special Branch, interviewed Detective Inspector George Davies about Kang. Afterward, in a private meeting with your predecessor and the then Foreign Secretary, a political decision was made not to tell SIS about Kang and his crimes because of his value to us as a source of intelligence." Roberts repeated, "It was a political, realpolitik decision in the interests of the UK.". "I know," Lewis looked cross, "but what to do now?" she added, "Nothing; all is still quiet, and our martyr won't get his justice." Lewis looked mistrustful but said her goodbyes and left the museum to go back to the foreign secretary with news of this looming political threat.

It took a day for Sarah Lewis to set up the meeting with the Foreign Secretary, Daniel Carver, and when it did take place, it was in the home of the Cabinet Secretary herself. Daniel Carver was a man in his early fifties but with fast greying hair and a slight belly paunch; he also had a battered face brought about by the years of being foreign secretary, the only secretary of state to keep his job in numerous reshuffles. "What's this about Sarah?" "It is about the alpha file. I sent you a brief yesterday; we need to talk about it." Carver looked at the cabinet secretary and remembered the brief, "Do you honestly think the former policeman will push looking for Kang?" Lewis thought for a moment and then answered, "Maybe, but that is not our major problem; we must make sure that the Special Branch report written must not come to light because your predecessor made a political decision that reflected his importance to the UK; consequently, the possibility that Kang was a serial killer was to be buried.". Carver looked at Lewis, put his hands to his temples, and asked, "How did this come to light in the first place?"

"Special Branch ran some checks and came up with the fact he may be a serial killer; the actual evidence was a letter we intercepted. It was written by Kang's boss in Hong Kong, Colonel Chen Li. He said Kang had been on several pickups, and on all of these occasions, he had returned late, and women had been murdered in the area he was meant to be; also, the letter contains a witness statement. Apparently, someone saw him kill one of the victims; the witness was a security officer attached to watch Kang.".

CHAPTER 10

Carver looked at Lewis. "So it was decided not to tell SIS, and they did not find out." "No, they did not; we kept it from them by suppressing records." "It was not too difficult," Lewis added. Carver contemplated what had been said and then tried a new tack: "But was there no moral consideration that SIS should be told"? "After all, having a mass murderer on your books is not, probably, a good ea." Lewis looked at him with a look of disdain. "I told you it was realpolitik, a political decision made by a minister. "Carver tried one last angle: "But this letter and Chen's knowledge surely the Chinese knew about it all. "Lewis looked at him and thought him weak and someone full of moral outrage, but only as long as votes were not involved. She spoke: "No, they did not. Chen only wrote one letter, which we grabbed through an agent. That was not the direct intention; the letter was purely accidental to the main target of that operation. Chen also was recalled in disgrace because of consorting with a prostitute working with the CIA; however, he committed suicide before he left, rumours being he was to be shot on arrival in Beijing.". Carver looked and listened, eventually saying, "Well, all we got to think about is this Davies chap." "We can deny everything, of course," Lewis was confident. "Good, do that." With that, Carver stood up and, thanked Sarah Lewis for her hospitality and left.

The sun rose over Edgefield that morning with a brightness that was turning from spring warmth to the heat of an early summer. Two months had passed since Kang had arrived in the UK; the debriefing had been going on every day, and Kang had been questioned over everything the

British could think of. Now, today he was to get a special visitor; the British called the visitor a "cousin." Kang was mystified...

The cousin was, in fact, James Alonso, CIA Liaison Officer to MI6. He had worked in London for five years, the last year as direct contact between the two intelligence services. He was American/Mexican Mother being Mexican and father being an American with roots in Chile, South America. He was of a big build, having played American football for the USAF and now rugby union for the Hounslow Harriers. As he was living in Hounslow now, he had his mother's looks, brown eyes, and a crew cut of his raven hair. He was 44 years old. His clothing this day was informal: corduroy trousers and a shirt, as the interview he was to conduct was to be in the dining room with Alonso asking and Kang answering, Alonso relying on the recording that Mrs. Donald would make. Alonso also had a special brief, but this was to wait until he could find out if the cousins knew the truth about Kang.

The dining at Edgefield was small, with sideboards and cabinets on one side and a wall full of paintings on the other. Mrs. Donald had arranged coffee, and it was laid out on the table, Alonso waiting for Kang, who had absorbed all of this. Kang came in, sat down, and stared at the American. "Good morning, Colonel Kang. Nice to meet you." Kang said nothing but instead poured out two cups of black coffee, keeping Alonso in view. Alonso was beginning to wonder about where things were going, as even though the interview was less than five minutes old, Kang was not going to play. He need not have worried; Kang opened. "You are, "he asked, "Alonso CIA," came the reply. "You're here to talk to me about American activities in Britain." "Yes," Alonso confirmed. Kang followed up, "Good, but first tell me why the USA and UK call each other cousins." "Then I answer questions; I'm curious to know." Alonso thought and then spoke: "Sir Guy Carlton was a governor of Quebec. He caught the patriots and tried to convince them they were wrong; he could not, so he told London they were no longer brothers but were now first cousins. That was the story as to why we call each other cousins".

Kang nodded his interest, then Alonso said, "Alright, tell me about Chinese activity against the United States in the UK." Kang looked at the American and said nothing, just gazing, seemingly deep in thought or not even concentrating on the room; eventually, he spoke: "I do not know any activities carried out by China against the United States in the UK." He went on, "I can tell you this because my superior officer, General Han Cheng, was wholly responsible for the Americans; it was his section; no one else was allowed to operate against the USA unless they had or were to be chosen by Han to work for him. I was responsible for the UK, nothing else. "But what if Han wanted to find out about Anglo-American cooperation and he needed help? Alonso's question was designed so an answer would come out that Kang knew something. "To answer that question, Han Cheng would simply put in a request for whatever he needed to know; he would never divulge anything or cooperate unless he had to; even then, he would always try to find out by himself.".

Alonso saw another chance and took it. "But surely then you had meetings to discuss such things." "No, never. "Kang was getting obstinate, and Alonso still did not wholly believe him. Kang, however, killed the line of questioning; he looked at Alonso again and said, General Cheng had a spy in SIS".

Alonso was staggered; he stared at Kang and thought quickly. The voice-activated tape had recorded everything, and so there was no problem there. He asked Kang the obvious, "Does Harvey know?" "No," said Kang. "I have not told them; I thought they knew, as I had passed information like that before. Alonso said, "I'm bringing Harvey in. I want you to tell him." "All right." Kang looked impassive despite his shattering news. Alonso said nothing, got up and left.

He got back to his car, then remembered his other brief about the Hong Kong women, but he had forgotten; it would have to wait; after all, surely the Brits knew what he thought.

CIA Headquarters, Langley, Virginia, one week before James Alonso had expected to be in London, but instead, he had been called in to see a deputy director of operations. He was sitting at a table looking at a bear of a man far bigger than him with blue eyes and blonde hair, with the name General Alexander Dubois.

"Sorry for the delay, but we have had an unexpected problem with the Chinese guy the cousins have got." "That's why I am here, thought Alonso, waiting for the punchline. "Here, look at these." The General passed a file inside five photos of murdered women. "What's this?" Alonso was curious. "The Brits have a serial killer on their hands. We got the information from a Hong Kong source before asking from a Hong Kong source. That's all you need to know". "OK, so what do you want me to do?" Alonso prepared for a long list. "First find out what Kang knows about us. Second, find out if he is a serial killer. Third, find out what the Brits know and what they don't". Alonso acknowledged his tasks and left to go home and then catch his new flight.

THE PRESENT, LONDON

Horton and Harvey were reviewing Kang's case. The interview went well, and Kang did not run, but both men were still worried by the suddenness of Kang's arrival in the UK. They had noticed during the debriefings that when he was asked about the decision to defect, Kang had stopped and been quiet in between questions. "He is hiding something, but what?" Horton thought aloud. "Well, the only thing to do now is to see what's going on in Beijing; I must check the latest reports." Harvey sat back in his chair, whiskey in hand.

CHAPTER 11

In Beijing it was 10 pm, and Ji Wu was in a blazing mood. When the body of his mistress had been found, it was General Han who it was believed to be the killer; now confirmation had arrived that it had been the defector Kang, and more to the point, there were ugly stories or rumours that Kang had done this before in Hong Kong. Now, General Han Cheng was imprisoned not for murder but for letting Kang escape that easily. However, it was the rumours that were the problem, a serial killer and a defector to boot; this could turn nasty for himself if it turns out Kang had killed female party functionaries.

The thing that Wu was angry over was the problem of Kang and how to solve it. Ideally, once a defector had gone, the losing country let the defector go, but Kangs's loss hurt, and there had to be a response. But how? Assassinating Kang seemed no longer a practical solution. "Robin" had panicked when Kang had appeared. So, Robin was no killer valuable where he was, but that was all. As for discrediting him, that was also a non-starter. The idea of creating a story to seed doubt in the mind of SIS was no longer tenable—not after the news of the mistress and her death. The British would be on their guard then because Kang had probably not told them. Wu thought, if that was the case, the British would have to review the entire thing, and that would take months, if not years, so Kang would have made his prison; no need then for Wu to act on anything. Wu smiled as this dawned on him.

The second option was already disposed of. Killing Kang had been an idea, and it was obvious Robin would be the assassin. Unfortunately, Robin had proved that his nerve was bad. Wu had also thought of "jenny," but this was also not good. First, if the British discovered "Jenny" and her identity, then there was the risk of having the entire embassy thrown out, as had happened to the Russians in 1971, Operation Foot 105 Russians thrown out of the UK. If that happened to us today, Wu thought the entire embassy would be shut. There was lastly "Jennys" contact, Chris Edward, but here too, there was a problem; true enough, Wu knew Edward was a dedicated communist, but was he dedicated enough to die for a cause? Wu did not believe so. Besides, Edward would have to be recruited trained and indoctrinated enough to want to kill Kang. That would take time, and time was something Wu was short on, as he had been to a politburo meeting, and the opinion was that Kang must not be allowed to live in peace. Wu had a lot to think about. Little did he know that in a few hours the entire thing would start to unravel spectacularly.

It had been days since George Davies had seen Peter Roy, and he was still in a deep rage followed by depression at what Roy had said and he, Davies, should about it. The truth was he did not know; he had come to what it seemed to be a dead end. No more case all over. But Davies still hurt, still felt bad at his failure over Hong Kong. He had to decide what to decide. Then he had what he thought was a remarkable idea. He remembered a junior civil servant in the governor's office just before the handover; he remembered she worked with both the police and Special Branch. Where was she, he thought? She had sent him a Christmas card in 1996; she would have been about 22 then, but still, it was a shot, and if she was still in the same part of London as the address on the card said. George wondered where the card was; he went to find it.

Davies had been at home in Hampshire, in London, where what was soon to be known as the battle of the "Middle Mews" was about to take place. In Britain, a stable or carriage house was built before the appearance of cars; they had living quarters above them. In the twentieth century, these buildings were adapted as homes. Andrew Harvey has such a place for his work, a place to interview people or hold meetings away from the world. Today, James Alonso, a CIA man, was the guest. Alonso had contacted Harvey and asked for a talk. Harvey had told him where and when and asked how important it was; should he bring Horton along? Alonso had said yes, that would be good. So today, all three men were sitting round a table.

Harvey started "Ok, Jimmy, what do you want to say?" Alonso looked at him; he knew how he played it: play it, don't be English, and go round the houses before the explanation; he would go straight in. "Your Chinese guy, Kang, is a serial killer." Both Horton and Harvey looked stunned. It was Horton who spoke first. "Alright, tell us how you know this." Alonso travelled back to Langley; he remembered what he had been told: "We got the information from a Hong Kong source. That's all you need to know". He remembered he decided to find out more. As luck would have it, the moment Dubois had dismissed him, a secretary arrived and took the file. Alonso had followed her out and, in the hallway, had brushed against her, knocking the two pieces of paper in the file to the floor. Alonso knelt down and quickly picked them up and handed them to the startled woman. "I'm sorry, my fault." "No, it happens," said the woman who Alonso found out was called Amanda. More importantly, he had read about the contact, a Chinese pro-democracy supporter who wrangled his way to work for the Hong Kong authorities but was giving secrets to anyone pro-Hong Kong. He had given his information to an American correspondent, who had realized the potential of the Kang story. He had given it to a magazine; the magazine editor had given it to a CIA contact as a piece of "information for the record.".

Alonso came back from his mind trip to the present and Harvey's home. The revelation that Kang was a serial killer of 6 women in Hong Kong still left Harvey, looking incredulous, Horton still said nothing. Harvey frowned and spoke: "Well, how did you find this out, and we did not?" "A Chinese prodemocracy contact as to why you were not told, we don't know; we assumed you had Kang tagged." "We did not." Harvey's voice Grew more aggressive, "You should have told us because you had information about our source." Horton interrupted, "James did say that it was a recent thing; sometimes this can't be helped." Harvey glared at him, "Bloody hell, Robert, do you realize what this means? We were to have resettled Kang in the community after we finished with him; now it seems we have a serial killer. That would look good in the newspapers if he were active." Horton nodded his head; he could imagine the tabloids if Kang was such a man, and they found out where he had come from and why.

It was Alonso who asked the inevitable, "What are you going to do?" "Well, first, talk to the foreign secretary to find out where we can deal with Kang and what is going on," and "second, find out from Kang himself." Harvey had thought quickly; he knew this problem to be sorted and sorted now. "Right, gentlemen, I suggest we get to it, and I suggest a meeting with the politicians.

Sarah Lewis had had a bad afternoon, and it was soon going to get worse. First, George Davies rang; it was a shock that Davies had found her, and she did admit to remembering him through his wife, who she was friends with. Yes, she knew the case. No, she could not help, and it was astonishing that Davies still had material; Lewis told him that there was also no one of that description here, and it was a mistake. Davies had argued, but Lewis stuck to his ground, and eventually, he put the phone down.

The second Was Harvey. It was the call that the Permanent Secretary to the Cabinet feared. Harvey had explained what had happened and that he wanted a meeting with the foreign secretary and, as a sideline, the commander of counterterrorism, who had access to old records. He also mentioned the CIA was going to be there. Lewis rang the foreign secretary's office. She did not sleep well that night.

CHAPTER 12

The Parish of Chevening is in Kent, a county in Southeast England notable for fruit and hop growing and as the cockpit of the Battle of Britain in 1940. It is like thousands of other parishes in England, except it contains Chevening House, the country residence of the foreign secretary. It was here on Wednesday morning that six people met. Sarah Lewis had organized the meeting with herself, the foreign secretary, and the Commander of Counter Terrorist Command. For the opposition, as it was seen, Harvey, Horton, and Alonso. The foreign secretary started: "Welcome everybody, and please help yourself to tea or coffee." The party made its way to the laid and buffet and helped themselves, no waiters or waitresses as the meeting was strictly private. The party was soon settled with tea or coffee, and the foreign secretary started the ball rolling: "This meeting was called to discuss new information regarding Colonel Lin Kang, lately of the Chinese Ministry of State Security and now a refugee in British care." Harvey looked at him and snapped back. "No, we are here to discuss why the SIS, of which I am the director, was not given information that would have altered our attitude; someone decided not to tell us.".

"Quite so, said the foreign secretary, Sarah. What do we know?" He looked at the Cabinet Secretary with expectations. Lewi knew the cue; she had discussed it with him before the meeting they were going to hang Chief Superintendent Allan Roberts out to dry. "The former Special Branch, now Counter Terrorist Command, advised us that it was advisable that, as Kang was an employee of the Chinese security service, he should be left alone to avoid a diplomatic incident, you know." Harvey exploded, "Bloody hell, Sarah, are you telling me that he was allowed to run free, even when he came to us?" "Yes, he was too valuable to us as a spy." Lewis did not show any emotion at all. Harvey turned to Roberts; he was by now livid. "What right do you have to dictate policy operations to us, and why not inform us in the first place?" Harvey's words were sharp and pointed, and Roberts, too, like Lewis, remained unshakeable: "We took the decision based on circumstances and diplomatic relations; at the time of discovery, we were in delicate negotiations over the nineteen ninety-seven handover."

"You're a bloody policeman." Harvey roared at Roberts, "You have no right." The foreign secretary intervened. "It was a political decision; it was the previous incumbent of my post who made the decision in the circumstances. It was unfortunate that Kang wanted to work for us, but these things can't be helped; besides, it was Mr. Alonso with the rest of the cousins who alerted us to our knowledge." Carver looked at Alonso, and Alonso looked back, thought for a second, and said, "The United States is not and cannot be responsible for British government foreign policy; we only acted in good faith as one allied power does for a friendly power." Carver and Roberts stared; Alonso had said his piece, and that was that; he was to say no more.

Now, there was silence in the room; the outburst of anger was over. Everybody stared at everyone else. It was Horton who had not spoken to break the stony silence. "Well, we will have to plan a new course. Andrew, you did say we must find out from Kang himself. Harvey thought and answered, "Alright, we deal with Kang next." Carver then interrupted, "Anything else, anyone? "Sarah Lewis glanced at Roberts, Roberts catching her glance, and spoke up. "There may be a former detective, George Davies, who was the investigating officer into the case in Hong Kong. He has retired now but found out about Kang through the newspapers; he wants to find Kang and bring him to justice." "Is there a chance this may happen?" Carver asked. "No, not at all." Roberts confirmed, "There is no problem.". Carver suggested; Roberts smiled, but deep down, he was angry with Harvey's remarks.

The party broke up, SIS and CIA went back to Edgefield, and the politicians and Counter Terrorist Command went back to London. Both were having conversations; the SIS and CIA were in deep conversations. "You should do the interview, James; you were the one with the facts at your fingertips." "Yeah, ok, I will do it." The American sat back in the seat and said, "Out of interest, have you thought about what you want to do with Kang after debriefing?" "Well, if it is all true, Kang will have to spend the rest of their time under our supervision. I can't imagine anything else, to be honest." Alonso was looking thoughtful. "What is it, Jimmy?" Horton had noticed. "Well, we in the U.S. have a lot of hiding places to put him out of the way; perhaps we should take him after you have finished with him." "That may be a good idea," Horton interjected, probably the best solution." Harvey did not answer but remained silent.

In the other car, there was, in fact, a similar conversation. "What's going to happen to Kang?" Carver asked. "He will be debriefed, and once that is done, he will get a new identity, a home, and a pension, and he will disappear, even though we keep an eye on him." Roberts laid out the plan. "How much of an eye?" Sarah Lewis quizzed the detective. "Regular checks and contact but no direct control." Lewis listened to Roberts and said, "So if he is what the American says he is, then he is a serial killer, and we must take extra precautions. Can we prosecute for Hong Kong?" "Unlikely," Carver pushed into the conversation. "Politics we would have divulged everything, not good for anyone." "So, it is best to wait for SIS and CIA," Carver summarized; everybody thought that was the best idea.

George Davies was despondent; he was downhearted and near his wits end. He had hit brick wall after brick wall. What to do now? He had no idea, absolutely none; he had apparently run out of options. He tried to contact his old boss, Detective Chief Inspector Paul Rodman, but Rodman had died in an accident in 2022. Car accident, so his widow said. So, what was to be done? Davies, sitting in the corner of the pub he was occupying, ordered another pint.

All this had taken place by midday in Britain; in China, it was 8 pm, and Ji Wu had had an informative day and had, because of this, directly formatted a plan to put before the Politburo. The first piece of information was that Colonel Lin Kang was the prime suspect in the murder of General Cheng's mistress. It had been thought it was Cheng, but the investigator had begun to believe it was Kang after DNA was finally realized proving Kang's guilt, so Kang had a reason to flee, Wu thought. The second piece of information was that Kang had killed in Hong Kong 6 times: a ticket collector, an air hostess, a policewoman, and a cleaner in a hotel, and the mistress, the sixth one, was a British female army officer forced to work for China under the threat of exposure as a lesbian. Wu was satisfied; his plan was quickly worked out. It was known that the Politburo wanted the traitor executed, and the only way to do that was to bring him back to China, and the way to do that was to accuse the British of hiding a known criminal and wanting him back. And once returned, he would be executed. The trick would, of course, be to manipulate the British media and thus humiliate the government into returning Kang.

Wu looked at the plan and was satisfied. He rang the personal aide to the president and made a request for a Politburo meeting. In due course, he got his meeting, and he got his request. Wu started "operation Collect" within a day of the meeting.

The following day in Britain, George Davies received a package with some very valuable information in it. It was to change everything and lead him to his target. In London, Chief Superintendent Allan Roberts was relaxing and feeling that this would be the last time the SIS chief interfered in Counter Terrorist Command business.

CHAPTER 13

The package that Davies received was a large one. It contained a letter on A4 lined paper with no address, no date, and no signature. The other thing in the package was a file about Kang. It told everything, including a sixth killing, which Davies had no idea about. He read the file and knew that he held in hand the best chance to catch Kang or, if not, to make the entire position difficult for the government.

Davies had received the package by courier at 9 am that morning; a few hours later, Kang was sitting at a table in Edgefield's dining room. On the other side of the table was Alonso with Harvey. Horton was out of sight, working the automatic voice recorder. Beforehand, it had been agreed that Alonso would conduct the interview. "This is the interview of Colonel Lin Kang, 25th May 2023, time 2 pm, present Andrew Harvey, head of SIS; Robert Horton, case officer; James Alonso, CIA; James Alonso, conducting the interview." Alonso did the introductions as a formality for the tape, then asked Kang, "You are Colonel Lin Kang, formerly of the Chinese Ministry of State Security; answer for the tape, please." "Yes, I am," Kang replied with a firm voice.

Alonso continued, "We wish to interview you over your time in Hong Kong, namely the time period 2nd July to 11th August 1995; during this time, six women were murdered, and we know you were in the area and that you killed them.". Alonso hoped the direct approach would work, and it would catch Kang out. Kang just stared and said nothing. Alonso repeated his words, "Six women were murdered, and we know you were in the area and that you killed them." Six women were murdered, and we know you were in the area and that you killed them. Kang, this time visibly winced, looked at Harvey and said, "No. "We have evidence, Colonel; we know it is good information." Alonso waited for a response. He watched Kang begin to sweat, and as he sat there, he began to see the vision of his sister, being held down on a table by two policemen. She was naked; a third was raping her. In the corner was the female captain directing the attack, watching impassively as the victim cried and screamed out in pain. Kang felt the rage he always did when he thought of his sister; he felt his stomach churn, his temperature rise, his fists turn into balls, and the desire to lash out...

Kang lunged at Alonso, but in that second, a side door flew open, and Jimmy smashed Kang off his chair and had a headlock on Kang in a second. Roger, at the same moment, had a Colt 45 pointing directly at Kang's temple. Harvey took control of the situation; in his most condescending tone, he admonished Kang, "Now colonel, be a good gentleman and please behave. I had Jimmy and Roger wait just in case such a thing as this should happen.". Jimmy lifted Kang back on the chair and stood behind him. Roger stood a little further back, the gun now holstered.

Harvey and Alonso looked at Kang; he looked defeated, crushed, as though a weight had been dropped on him and then lifted. Alonso spoke: "Now, Colonel, the truth, please." Kang put his head in his hands and, to the astonishment of all there, began to cry. He cried uncontrollably. He looked at the others, tears streaming down his face. Harvey eventually found a handkerchief and gave it to Kang, who wiped his face. Some minutes passed; it was Kang who broke the silence. "Yes, I did it; I killed all of them," he went on, "including number six.". "Tell me about number six," Alonso gently urged.

Kang looked at him and then looked round the room, looking for a friendly face, but there was no one; just the glares of Jimmy and Roger, the staring gaze of Harvey, and the questioning look of Alonso. Eventually, Kang told them. "We found Captain Sarah Jones in a disco; we had no idea until one of the talent spotters took a chance and found out who she was." "So, it was a random chance, not a chosen one." Harvey, while speaking, leaned forward to give Kang the impression he was interested, which he was. "Yes, totally. It took two weeks to work out who she was. When we found out she was army intelligence, we decided to move. When we discovered her liking for women, we set the trap." "How long did she work for you, and when did you kill her?" Alonso now took the lead again. Please tell us.".

Kang looked at his questioner, put his head in his hands, took a deep breath, and told his story: "She worked for us for about six months; she gave personnel files and information on movements of diplomats, soldiers, and politicians; she could get her hands on nearly everything we asked for." Kang waited for a response; he saw Alonso make a note, and then Alonso looked at him. "Now tell us how she died." Alonso looked at Kang and stared. Kang felt Alonso lock on and, in the hope of breaking eye contact, blurted out, "I killed her during our second pickup meeting at a safe house in the New Territories; where in the New Territories?"Alonso was pursuing the prey with relish. "Sha Tin District," Kang answered in a quiet tone, then continued, "She was in her uniform and had a jacket over the top.". Kang went on, "We sat down, and they gave me a package. It was a set of personnel files with the names of senior officials coming to the Colony." "Then what happened?" Alonso pressed and pressed hard; there was a hurriedness in his speech. "I saw her uniform, felt a rage, and felt nothing. I grabbed her round the throat and strangled her. "Kang paused. Alonso stared; Kang got the message and went on, "I tore at her clothes until she was naked; I then knew I must dispose of the body, so I put her in my car, drove to the container port car park, then took the body from the car and dumped it in a bin." "That's where we found her, "Alonso interjected. "Why weren't the police informed?" Harvey suddenly became acute to the questioning. "The special branch was, no need to tell the local police, Kang parked in a restricted area of the container port; also, a video camera caught Kang coming and going, and with the victim, "Alonso explanation mollified Harvey; now he understood my Special Branch had acted in the way they did." Then Harvey, after a couple of seconds, added, "That could have been our area of expertise." "No deal." Alonso explained the entire thing became political with the murder and the fact the killer was a serving agent and Hong Kong was being handed back; the need for a tidy deal was essential.

During these exchanges, Kang sat on his chair with his head in his hands; he was listening and taking everything in. Eventually, once Harvey had finished, Kang asked, "What is going to happen to me?" There was silence; a pin could have dropped and resounded with a crash. Finally, Harvey told the Chinese defector, "We will have to see what to do; you have given us a difficult problem. Harvey then said, "I think we should retire to think things through." Alonso nodded, and Kang looked crushed. Soon, Kang was back in his room, and the three intelligence officers were talking. "I think we need a psychiatrist; we really need to know about Kang. " Harvey's words hit the mark: Alonso volunteered to speak to a psychiatrist who was attached to the US embassy. Alonso said the Dr. could be there in two days. Harvey and Horton nodded their agreement.

Upstairs Kang was deep in thought; he was very afraid the British would return him to China. Then what? He did not know what to do or say; would he be tried here? He did not know. He then had an idea; he must rely on his own resources; he would plan to escape soon.

CHAPTER 14

Kang's interview was on Thursday. On Saturday, Alonso brought the psychiatrist as promised. She was a Daphne Stewart of the George Washington Memorial Hospital, now of the medical staff of the US embassy in London. Alonso made the introductions: "Robert, Andrew, this is Daphne, the doctor I told you about." "Nice to meet you, Daphne, both men said. "Nice to meet you." The reply was instantaneous.

The doctor followed up: "Where is the patient?" "Upstairs," Alonso said, and leading the way, he took the doctor to Kang; on the way, Jimmy and Roger arrived, Alonso assigning them to the doctor with instructions to keep an eye on Kang during the interview. He need not have worried; the interview went well. Kang answered all of Dr. Stewart's questions and told her about his sister.

Downstairs, Dr. Stewart delivered her opinion: "In very simple layman's terms, Kang has a personality disorder and is a sociopath, brought about by what happened to his sister and the breakdown afterward of his family and his work in the Ministry of State Security." "What family breakdown, and what work?" Harvey sounded incredulous; he added, "Kang said nothing." "He would not have the memory buried deep; he tried to forget." Dr. Stewart recrossed her legs, lit a cigarette, and waited for the next question. Harvey looked at her and was about to comment on the non-smoking rule in the house but thought better of it when recrossing her legs; Harvey thought he saw a naked vagina. However, he could not be sure, so he asked, "What do we do now, and what was this about his family?" Stewart Looked at him and thought eventually, she answered, "Well, he needs to be sent to a mental health unit. It may have to be a place like Broadmoor." She continued. "As for his family, the police took them all away the following day. Kang was sent home three days later, and the following his elder sister, no sign of the parents until years later when Kang found out by accident that they had been shot the day they were arrested; the mother, of course, had been abused beforehand. As for his further service, it just made him worse because of the interrogations he took part in.

All four sat quietly, wondering; finally, it was Horton who spoke: Well, it's a hospital then when we have finished. "We must make him disappear. The meeting agreed and broke up.

Kang was sitting on his bed and was thinking of his escape. He has been thinking all day about his escape. He had no real idea; wherever he went, he had Jimmy or Roger or both with him. He was never alone; apart from the night, even then, his bodyguards shared guard duty in the hallway outside. But there had to be a way...

THE EDITORS OFFICE "POLITICS WEEKLY"

David Samuelson was fed up; he had had a bad day, first with having to deal with a case of libel. One of his journalists had written a piece accusing a conservative MP of being an active communist, using his conservatism as a" false flag," meaning he was pretending to be something he was not and working in an organization he did not believe in. The second one was that his daughter had been caught in a drug bust at a party.

Consequently, his partner, the girl's mother, had been snapping at him all day about his liberal attitude toward the social use of drugs. Now had this guy Chris Edward, telling a weird story about a serial killing defector. The "guy" said, "What do you think?" He went on, "I think it would do good in your magazine, a piece about reactionary forces ignoring the law." Edward knew that the magazine was left-wing; he also knew that if the article was published, it would make no difference to the magazine and its fortunes, but the readership was partly made up of freelance investigative journalists, and one of these would surely bite.

Samuelson looked at his visitor; his tired voice spoke again, "One more time, just let me hear it one more time.". So, Edward repeated the story: Kang's time in Hong Kong, his treachery to China, and his murder that led to his flight. He finished and waited for Samuelson. Samuelson looked thoughtful and then said, "You want me to publish and then hope a journalist for one of the dailies gets the story." Chris Edward could only nod in agreement. Samuelson said, "Listen, I will publish, but we run with the story if it strikes a vein and someone gets rattled." Chris nodded again. "Alright, we publish and run. Where did you say this place was called again?" "Edgefield," came the reply. "Alright, we go; talk to you when we are ready to publish." Samuelson got up, opened the door, and let Edward out and followed him; he needed to talk to Adanna Ado Macdonald.

"That would be five pounds, sir." The barman handed George Davies his whiskey, and Davies, standing at the bar, looked down into it, the barman noticing, said, "Is everything ok, sir?" Davies looked at him and, realising he must have been seen pondering, answered, "Yes, I find thanks, but one thing." "What's that, sir?" The barman became interested as the stranger was brightening a slow day. Davies continued, "The house just outside the village Edgefield, I think it's called, who lives there or what happens there." The barman thought and replied, "I have no idea; you see, I don't live here, but Rosie does. She'll tell you. The barman called her name, and soon, a woman with a large build and red hair flowing to the waist appeared. Davie made a mental note that she could have easily fallen out of the seventeenth century, such was her build and style.

Davies introduced himself as an amateur historian with an interest in old houses, and he wanted to know about Edgefield. "It's a government property agricultural research or some such." Rosie filled in the story as far as she could; she had grown up around here, and the house, as far as she knew, had always been government property. Davies thanked her for her time, drank his whiskey, and decided to take a walk. He turned to go, and as he approached the exit, the door was opened. Davies went to hold it open just as a small Black woman with short, cropped hair and wearing a pair of torn jeans and a bright blue t-shirt pushed against the door and him. "I'm so sorry," Davies, in the traditional English way, put his apology in first. "It's alright," the woman said, and with that, George Davies and Adanna Ado Macdonald passed each other without a care in the world for the other.

Kang was wrestling on his bed; he could not rest; he had to think of a way out; he was convinced he would be returned to China and executed at the airport once he arrived back on Chinese soil. He thought further surely there was something he had missed, or the British had missed, but he could think of nothing. He would have to think more.

Adanna Ado Macdonald had just finished her lunch. She had a glass of wine to finish; it had been a trip down from London to here, and she was pleased to eat. She remembered what David Samuelson had told her. "You will travel to Edgefield and stay in the motel there. The house, the village, and the motel are within five minutes of each other. You will try and catch a glimpse of this man, Kang, take a photo, and come home and write the story." Adanna thought about all this and decided to try and take a sneak photo, probably with a long-range lens. She took another sip of wine and considered her options. She did not have many; she knew about the house, unlike George Davies, she had been told by Samuelson. She also knew it would be dangerous as Edgefield was no agricultural research station. She took another sip of the red wine she ordered; she saw her reflection in the glass, a product of a Black Congolese mother and a white Scottish father, born in East Germany to communist student parents, and when the Berlin Wall came down, her father took his wife and baby Adanna to Scotland, getting out of the way of a West German government looking into war crimes at the Berlin.

Wall because her father had betrayed several people wanting to leave the "workers' paradise."

CHAPTER 15

While Adanna was having lunch, George Davies had taken himself off to Edgefield to have a look at the house. When he got there, he looked around and looked at the environment. The entrance to the house was on the main road, but you could not see the house, just the driveway. The entrance itself was decorated by two greyhounds mounted on pedestals. There was also a wall that obviously went round the estate; the driveway bisected the wall. There was also a sign that said, "EDGEFIELD AGRICULTURAL RESEARCH STATION GOVERNMENT PROPERTY KEEP OUT. Davies had to plan to leave it or go further; he decided to go on.

He crossed the road, went past the greyhounds, and walked down the driveway; he could not see the house as he approached a right bend in the driveway, and a skinny white man suddenly appeared from behind a tree. "What do you want?" said the skinny man. "My name is George Davies. I have an interest in old houses like Edgefield; I like to have a look." The skinny man, or Roger, as he was known to the house, thought for a moment and then pulled a walkie-talkie from his pocket and pushed a button. Moving away from Davies, he spoke into it. "Sentry 1 to base, sentry 1 to base," "Come in, Sentry 1, what have you to report?" Horton had answered the call. "I have a man here who says he has an interest in the house; he says he has a historical interest in the house." "Sentry 1 base here; tell him to speak to Mrs. Donald in the village about the house. "Roger base out." Roger put the walkie-talkie away and turned to Davies. "Sorry, sir, if you want to find out about the house, you must speak to Mrs.

Donald in the village." Davies looked at Roger and suddenly noticed the bulge under his T-shirt. A gun, Davies thought. He quickly made his apologies and promised to speak to Mrs. Donald. Clearly, Edgefield had secrets that needed to remain well hidden. From his window, Kang had seen the whole showdown and had seen a potential escape route, and now all he needed was a chance or opportunity.

Soon after Davies had been sent away, Roger saw a second would-be visitor, a Black lady, small but walking purposefully down the road, heading to the driveway of Edgefield. Roger watched; the woman took no notice of any of the signs and walked down the driveway. Adanna also could not see the house as she approached a right bend in the driveway; on cue, Roger appeared, but this time Adanna was ahead of the game; she noticed the pistol bulge, but instead of withdrawing, she said, "For a research station, why do you need to be armed?" Roger was momentarily unbalanced by the remark but quickly recovered and angrily demanded, "Who are you, and what do you want?" Adanna stayed calm, explaining who she was, who she worked for, and that she wanted to see the manager. Roger went through the walkie-talkie procedure again: "Sentry 1 to base, sentry 1 to base," "Come in, sentry 1, what have you to report?" Horton again answered the call. "I have a woman who wants to talk about the agricultural station." In the control room, Horton froze; the term "the agricultural station" meant that someone had got the idea of what was really going on at Edgefield; that meant trouble, and it had to be nipped in the bud fast. "Horton, here, bring the visitor to the front door, and I will meet you. I will deal with it." "Roger control," Roger replied, and putting the walkie-talkie away, he told Adanna, "This

way," and took Adanna to the front of the house where
Horton was waiting.

"Welcome to Edgefield, Miss—" "It is Ms." Adanna
quickly corrected Horton, who apologized and then said, "I
would like to show you around; we have nothing to hide, I
can assure you," Adanna said nothing, just smiled, and they
began the tour. Horton showed everything he was meant to:
the greenhouses, the field used for experimental crops, and
the research lab. He showed everything except the house. He
had hoped Adanna, as she was called a journalist, had not
noticed. But she had said nothing until she said the inevitable,
"What about the house?" Even though it was the inevitable
question, Horton still had to prepare a defense: "It is office
and living quarters for the staff, including me." Adanna
looked at him and said nothing. Horton felt nervous; this
woman had the skill of keeping her mouth shut until
necessary. They walked on until they reached the main road.
"Well, goodbye, Ms. Macdonald." Horton was deliberate in
his tone. "Before I go, Mr. Horton, I just want to say I don't
believe a word of what you said or what you do here."
Horton was staggered by the attack. Adanna went on, "I
believe you have a Chinese defector in there, a colonel in the
Ministry of State Security, and that he is a serial killer; further,
you are hiding him. If he is released after you finish with him,
women anywhere could be in trouble."

Horton was horrified but did not show it and denied it.
Adanna, seeing and sensing she had rattled the man, said
nothing except, "Goodbye, Mr. Horton." With that, Adanna
turned toward the Premier Inn and started walking. Horton
went back to the house, rang Harvey in London, and
explained the day's events. That evening, a policeman was on

guard at the entrance, and the following morning, new CCTV cameras were to be covertly set up near the main road. Harvey had got these going as he had seen the threat posed by the presence of this journalist. How had she got a lead? That was also a thing to deal with.

That had been the day before, and the next day then, CCTV people arrived; Bert Stanwick and his son. Paul. Horton met them in the hallway. "You know what's to be done: cameras on the drive, please." "Yes, we understand. It will take about three hours to set up. "Bert was already heading out to the point in the driveway. Kang had been sitting in the dining room when all that was taking place; he was thinking of escape, and now he saw a chance. With the CCTV being installed, perhaps the attention would slip from him, and he could make a dash for freedom.

Kang thought quickly; he would have to be soon; he quickly assimilated the situation. He and Roger were in the dining room. There was a door that led out onto the terrace, and then you could cross the lawn to the road. Jimmy, Horton, and Mrs. Donald were in various places in the house, and Jimmy would take time to catch up with him once he had started.

Kang then had to think about Roger; he knew when he left the dining room, Roger would be right next to him. He knew that escape was only possible if Roger was brought to a halt. Kang picked up a fork and put it in his pocket. "I'm ready to go, "Kang called out as Roger appeared; it occurred to Kang he could have gone before, but Roger was fast; he could have caught Kang quickly. Better this way, he thought.

Kang got up from the table and moved off; Roger was behind. They moved a few steps, and then Kang made his move; he took the fork from his pocket, and before Roger had properly seen it, Kang stabbed it into his leg. Roger fell, and Kang, remembering his training days, punched Roger in the face, which sent him on his back. Kang ran towards the door flung open, ran across the terrace, and toward the driveway. By now, Roger was recovering and pressed the alarm on his phone; soon, Jimmy was with him, and, seeing what had happened, chased after Kang. Kang had reached the driveway and, knowing he needed cover, had hidden in a ditch and covered himself when he heard the Nigerian voice alerting the world to the escape. Jimmy had, however, chosen the wrong direction, thinking Kang would avoid the road and was in the back amongst the research greenhouses.

CHAPTER 16

Kang had lain still, listening for anything. He guessed he must have waited for about fifteen minutes and heard nothing. He thought about the direction he knew he was near the village and civilization; he also knew the other direction would take him further from Edgefield. He lay and thought. Eventually, he decided he would go to the village, break into a house, and steal food, money, and clothes.

At Edgefield there was chaos; Roger was having his leg tended to by the doctor summoned by Horton, and Jimmy had reported Kang was nowhere in the grounds. Mrs. Donaldson was acting in her real role as security officer for Edgefield and was reporting the incident to Andrew Harvey. Harvey was not pleased. "Mrs. Donaldson Kang's escape is embarrassing; he must be found. Where could he have gone? Mrs. Donaldson shifted uncomfortably from one leg to the other; she answered, "He has a choice: the village or open country." Harvey listened and told the shaken woman, "He has gone to the village; he will need food, money, and clothes." "But what if he has not?" Mrs. Donaldson asked what seemed to be a logical question. "He has; he's there. Kang needs things like that before he makes his next move." Harvey was sternly talking to Mrs. Donaldson. Mrs. Donaldson acknowledged Harvey's idea and called Jimmy and two men who had "appeared" from the research team that was Edgefield's cover. Mrs. Donaldson addressed them: "Jimmy, take these two with you, go into the village, and look for Kang. If you can, bring him back here; if not, let us know, and we will sort it out.

Kang had been hiding in a greenhouse that belonged to the first house from the direction of Edgefield; he had no idea of time and space; he only knew he had to at all costs, keep moving. He watched the house and then took in the rest. To his left, another house and garden, and to his right, woodland. Kang looked straight ahead. He looked one final time; no one was around, so he opened the greenhouse door and sprinted towards the back door of the house. He reached the back door and pressed himself against the wall. He listened again. Nothing. Still, with his pressed against the wall, he moved towards the back door and laid his hands on the handle; the door was open, not locked; he pushed it open. Nothing was heard, he went inside. He found himself in a kitchen; he looked around. There was fruit and bread and butter on the table, and a shopping bag hung over the backrest of a chair. Kang quickly gathered the food and put it in the bag, then stopped again and listened to nothing. So, he went to the living room. He found nothing of use there; he went upstairs to the bedroom; that's where he would find clothes. He climbed the stairs and soon found the master bedroom. He listened to nothing, so he moved to the wardrobe. Opening the doors, he saw that a couple lived there, and the man was slightly bigger than Kang, but Kang did not mind that. That would have to do. He took a couple of suits and ties, a pair of jeans, a t-shirt, and a pair of shirts and underpants. He put them in a bag, which he found in the bottom of the wardrobe. It had shoes but no more.

Kang was about to go downstairs when he heard the noise. The noise of a key being turned in a lock. He froze. He heard it again, and this time footstep. He quietly went to the top of the staircase and looked over the banister; he saw the woman down below, and she had her back to him. Kang moved quietly back into the bedroom and hid the wardrobe. He listened; the woman was coming up the stairs.

He listened further, but the woman did not come into the bedroom. She walked past to another room, went in, and shut the door. Kang slowly, very slowly and quietly, opened the wardrobe door and crept out of the bedroom and towards the sound of someone dressing in the room opposite the bedroom. Kang knelt down and, with one eye, peered through the keyhole. He saw the woman naked, her clothes on the bed and another set hanging over a chair, but there was something else of interest, a handbag, and handbags meant money. Kang watched and waited. The woman got dressed first in black underwear and a bra, black tights, then dark blue trousers, then a white shirt. finally, a small tie. The woman turned around, and Kang saw she was wearing a woman police officer's uniform. Kang felt a sickness in his stomach and then felt the pain he got in his head and then the feeling of rage and hate, which built slowly but rose to a crescendo. Kang opened the door and went in; the woman with her raven black hair now in a bun stared in horror.

Kang stopped in front of her; the woman looked into his eyes but saw nothing, just a stare. Then Kang lunged, and he began tearing the clothes and hitting blows harder and harder each time. Then he grabbed around the throat and squeezed until the body flopped lifeless on the floor. Kang took the torn clothes off the body, threw them in a corner, picked up the handbag, and left. He had been gone thirty minutes when Tracey Shaw, with her baby boy Paul, visited the house; she found her sister, police sergeant Sophie Nichols, dead on the floor....

George Davies was in the pub again. He tried Mrs. Donaldson's home, but she was not at home, and he was trying to think of a new way of finding out about Edgefield's. He looked at his beer; he just had to wait until Mrs. Donaldson was at home or something came up. He heard police car sirens, then silence for a second; he wondered what was happening...

Adanna Macdonald was sitting in a picnic area. She had just finished talking to her editor, Samuelson. She had told him everything that had happened, and Samuelson had told her not to give up and that expenses incurred would be repaid in full. At that moment she too heard the siren, but unlike George Davies, her sense of a story was overwhelming; she got up and walked back to the village.

A third group had also heard the sirens; Jimmy and his two accomplices had been in the village quietly looking for traces of Kang. Jimmy had heard the sirens, and instinct told him that it must be Kang. So, he, too, went towards them. In the meantime, he called Horton and told him what had happened.

Horton listened to what Jimmy said and told him to find out as much as possible. Horton looked at his watch: 2 pm. Harvey had organized a Zoom meeting for 2:15 pm. Horton was to be there with Harvey, Alonso, Roberts from the special branch, and Dr. Daphne Stewart. Harvey started: "As you know, Colonel Ling Kang has escaped. As I explained before setting up this meeting, I brought you all together to discuss the next moves. At the moment, we are still looking.". Roberts spoke up. "I have put out feelers to find out more; if possible, I will let you know." Harvey thanked him. Alonso spoke next, "We can, of course, offer any assistance you need." Harvey then spoke to Dr. Stewart. "Dr. Stewart, you, as I see it, are the most important here, having interviewed Kang and having an idea of the man." "Well, yes, I do, and it is a dangerous situation." "How so?" Harvey asked. "Kang has a personality disorder; if he is having to look for food or whatever, he would kill again, this time to survive maybe. May I say if this was America, then by now a murder hunt would be launched?". "Well, he has not, as far as we know, committed murder," Horton interjected. Roberts then followed on "I," and on the screen, he was seen to take a phone call. His face showed nothing; he put the phone down. "I just heard from one of our officers, a woman, who was murdered in her home about an hour ago.". There was silence. The Dr. Stewart said, "I think we need a murder hunt.". "Can we be sure it was Kang?" Harvey asked. Roberts explained what had been taken and the MO. There could be very little doubt it was Kang.

CHAPTER 17

Earlier, outside Sophie Nichols's house, Detective Inspector Reid and Detective Sergeant Jones had arrived. Reid approached the uniformed officer on guard by the door. "The area is secured, and who found the body?" "Yes, the area is secure, and Sophie's sister found the body; she is inside, sir.". "Ok, let's get started. Sergeant Jones, go and see what the body is like, and I will talk to the witness.". "Yes, sir, Jones made his way upstairs, thinking and hoping the message he was going to send to the special branch would bring some action... He got to the bedroom, saw the body, recognized the pattern he had been told earlier, then talked to the officer on guard, got the details as known, and then went out of earshot and made his call.

Downstairs, Reid had spoken to the sister, who could only tell him how she had found Sophie on the floor naked, with a grotesque fear on her face. Reid listened and took notes, but there was nothing more to be done with the witness. At that moment he heard the officer at the door talking to men; Reid went to investigate. He found the constable with two men, a short, fat Black man and a man with blue eyes, skin that was worn, hair that was turning gray, and a man who had not seen a medical test or a gymnasium in years. The Black man was short with fat arms and what could only be described as a belly, clean-shaven; the only thing about him was his eyes, alert and always looking around. "What can I do for gentlemen?" "My name is Horton, and this is my assistant, James Okeke. Can we talk privately?" Horton waited for a response: "Know something about all this?" Reid knew the question was rhetorical. "Yes, said Horton. "Ok, we go to the car." With that, Ride led the way to his own car; he sat in the driver's seat, and Horton in the passenger seat, while Jimmy did not stay next to the car, watching ever so watchful. Horton told Reid what he should know; he left out the Zoom meeting, the fact Reid's sergeant had been the Zoom meeting's informant, and the real reason for Kang's presence in the UK, telling Reid that Kang was a diplomat caught with a prostitute and promoting Chinese students to spy for China and promoting violent student demonstrations that had happened recently. They also naturally left out the other murders. Now in custody, he was being worked on to work for the British before his escape, adding naturally that the escapee was violent. Ride listened carefully and, at Horton's suggestion, agreed to a murder hunt, with the proviso that Kang, after high-level negotiations, is handed to the Anti-Terrorist Command. Reid agreed.

At that moment, Horton saw the figure of a Black lady walking toward the car; he readied himself for trouble. Adanna approached the car; seeing Horton and the police and guessing Jimmy was Horton's man, she prepared to ask questions. Horton opened the side window. Hello, "Ms. Macdonald, what do you want to know?" "Tell me what happened. I see the police are everywhere, and your canvas barrier is up; something's going on. Someone's been murdered," Adana's bluntness rankled Horton's thoughts. It was Reid who saved Horton from a roasting: "Yes, it was a murder by a female police officer. You will hear more in due course." Reid stared hard at the journalist. Adanna answered, "Yes, okay, I will be at the press conference; see you later." With that, Adanna started to walk away. While walking, she telephoned her editor to tell him of her suspicion.

George Davies was on his way to try Mrs. Donaldson again. He reached the house and pressed the doorbell, but there was still no answer; they were still not at home. Davies turned to go when suddenly the next-door neighbor came out, "Looking for Mrs. D." Davies turned again to find out where the noise came from. He found himself looking at an Indian woman, "She still must be at the research station; she must be busy." The woman filled in the details before Davies could ask the question. "Do you know when she will be back?" Davies was able to say something in between the onslaught, "No, by the way, I am Sarah Rani." "George Davies," said Davies. "Sorry, I can't help anymore, but it has been a bit of a funny morning; I had the police earlier asking questions; there's been a murder in the village, well, according to village gossip." "Oh, do you know who?" Davies was making small talk as he had nothing more to do. "Well, gossip says she was a policewoman, about to go to work when she was killed," Davies listened and thought, and then he said, "Was she a detective?" "No, in uniform," came the reply. Davies's mind clicked there and then, and he turned to go. "Where is this house?" he asked. "Round the corner number—" but Davies had gone round the corner, heading for somewhere.

He soon found "Somewhere," and he saw who he thought was the investigating officer. Detective Inspector Reid also saw him; Davies opened the conversation. "Are you the investigating officer?" "Yes, I am Detective Inspector Reid looked at the new arrival, Davies, who continued, first pulling out his ID card from Hong Kong days, then saying, "I can help you with the investigation." I've seen this MO before, saying this Davies mind held firm in the pictures of Hutchison Park Hong Kong, 30th July 1995, and Constable

Sandra Wu, age 26. Read Looking at him with a strange look, Davies was wondering what his problem was. Reid finally spoke, "Alright, I'm listening.". Davies talked and told him everything, showing him the still photo from the Conrad Pacific Hotel murder. Reid said nothing, just looked. He still said nothing after giving the photo back. Davies broke the silence. "Do you want the photo?" "No, but I think you should know you're not the only one looking for Kang.". Reid explained the earlier events and waited for a reaction. He got it. "I want to see Kang arrested and brought to trial for this one if not for the Hong Kong killings." "Well, the statute of limitations has seen to that," Reid commented; besides, it has been agreed that after high-level talks, Kang goes back to SIS and Antiterrorist Command. Davies said nothing...

The barn was old and abandoned, like hundreds of others throughout the UK. Once a hive of activity, this one had long since seen use until today, when its one occupier had made himself at home for the night. With the summer sun setting outside, Kang made himself as comfortable as possible in his broken-roofed home. He was thinking about his next step. He thought he had to get to London, as once there he could disappear amongst the Chinese community. He looked out of a broken window; he could see the village and the police still coming and going. It was a bad idea to go back to the village; that left the alternatives: he leaves the barn, turns left, and goes back past Edgefield. That was stupid; he came out of the barn and, walked around to the back of the barn and walked on. That was also not good; it was just woodland, and he had no idea of the village. So, the only thing he could do was turn right from the barn door and walk, following the road from the village. He knew there was no alternative. He settled down to sleep.

At Edgefield, Horton Harvey, Alonso, Roberts, and Stewart were reviewing the day, and all were trying to work out Kang's next move. The men all looked to Dr. Stewart to open the batting, as Roberts called it. Alonso smiled at the description of how to start a conversation; using a cricket analogy, he could not help but add that so far, Kang had destroyed the SIS batting. Roberts did not find it funny. Harvey brought the meeting back to the main point: "Well, what's happening now then?" he asked. "Police are going to start a search at first light; the alert is going out on the evening news in an hour ", Horton explained. Harvey looked at his watch; it said 4 pm. "Good, then 6 pm news." "Aren't we being a little slow?" Alonso looked thoughtful. "No," said Roberts. "The boots on the ground are convinced our boy has not gone far." Harvey intervened, "Ok, then we wait for tomorrow." The trouble was tomorrow was not going to wait.

CHAPTER 18

The car pulled up the driveway. There were three people in it, two in the back and the driver. The Edgefield group was in the lounge, having had supper, and were now sipping drinks. It was Alonso who saw the new arrivals. "We expecting anyone?" "No." Harvey looked out the window as the car stopped, and the driver got out and opened the door; a woman of medium build and a tall rugby-playing type with short-cut brown hair; the woman was a peroxide blonde. The doorbell rang, and Horton moved to open the door. He opened the door, and the visitors stepped inside.

By now the rest of the group had joined, and Roberts made introductions: "This is Detective Chief Superintendent Thresa Jones and Chief Constable Jonathan Michaels." Roberts waited, expecting courteous formality, but instead, Micheals exploded, "What the bloody hell is the meaning of this, Roberts? What the hell are you people doing?". The shock of the verbal attack took everyone back, and it was Harvey that brought everything back on track. "What has happened? Perhaps we can straighten things out," "Good idea, "DCS Jones snapped. Harvey noted her mood was just as violent as Michaels's. He continued, "How can we help?" "By telling us the truth and nothing but the truth." "All right, let us exchange facts." Harvey Horton had noticed he had gone into diplomatic mode, behaving like a cat that ran round the owner's feet looking for attention when it wants a cuddle.

The chief constable explained what had happened when Horton had spoken to Reid, and then George Davies had spoken to Reid and left DI Reid with two different stories over the same man, but with a photograph produced by

Davies, which he now showed the assembled group: "Is this him?" he growled. "Yes, that is Kang," Roberts confirmed. Harvey added, Yes, the story is true, and we are sorry for the deceit, but it was a question of security over the Hong Kong events. "But still, we would have liked to know that we had a possible psychopath on our hands." "Actually, personality disorder," Dr. Stewart put her contribution in. "Oh, that's just great." DCS Jones looked annoyed; Michaels took the playback. "I think we should work together with no more secrets unless it is a national security issue.". "Agreed, everybody ok with that?" Harvey hoped to kill the argument there and then; he noticed they had not even moved from the hallway. No one said a word against it, and the enlarged group moved back for more drinks.

BEIJING 5 AM JI WU'S OFFICE

While drinks were being served at 9 pm, it was 5 am in Beijing, and Ji Wu was still working. He had heard of Kang's escape the previous day at 11 pm Beijing time and had spent the time following the story and thinking about what to do with the now-on-the-run defector. His plans had fallen apart, and now he had to report to the politburo in 4 hours' time. He had very little sleep and needed a brand-new plan. He had been thinking hard. What to do? Kang was on the run, and now it was an official murder hunt. He poured more coffee and lit another cigarette. He started smoking again since Kang had defected; now he was back to almost 40 a day. But what to do? There was only one thing for it.

He thought again about "Jenny." If she was caught with her false identity, then the entire embassy would be shut down and thrown out of the UK, and the consuls shut down as well. It was a very big risk, but with Kang on the run and a hunted man and "Jenny" being the only professional around, Wu knew he had very little choice. He drew up a plan for the Politburo to discuss; he called it operation "Qiang sheng, or gunshot.

Hours later, the sun rose over the barn that was Kang's home. It was 5:45 am; the sun woke Kang up; he looked out the window saw nothing, but expected the manhunt to begin. He looked into his bag and found the food. He took some water from a flask he had found, then looked in the handbag he had stolen. He found ladies things: lipstick, a mirror, tissues, a handkerchief, and more makeup. At the bottom he found the purse; he opened it. In one compartment there was cash, one hundred pounds; in another, a credit card and a debit card. The credit card would be no good, but the same compartment along with the cards had a slip of paper from the bank on which was written "YOUR NEW DEBIT CARD NUMBER." It went on to say never divulge the number and destroy this information at once. Kang could not believe his luck; the woman must have forgotten all about it; he had a money supply. He finished his meal, packed up, walked out of the barn, turned right, keeping the road in view, and started; the time was 6:15 am.

At the same time, Inspector Paul Knowsley was assembling his search parties; he was annoyed with the top brass; they had originally told him to search the village in case the killer was "a tree hiding in the woods." Now, he was being told that the suspect was highly dangerous and should not be approached by members of the public. He had also been told the suspect was well-trained and clever in the art of "disappearing," as he was quoted. He smiled, though when he had passed on the information to his sergeants leading the hunt, the common reply was, "Who we are looking for, Houdini." Knowsley assured them no, they were not.

He then sent out his searchers in groups: one group for the village, four groups for each of the compass points, and a fifth group for the woods around Edgefield and the old barn just outside the village. The group left at 6:25 am, and they reached the old barn at just after 6:35 am. They, of course, found nothing...

Ji Wu had come out of the meeting at 9:45 am. It had only taken forty-five minutes. His plan for the was discussed, and operation "Qiang sheng," or gunshot, was given permission to go ahead. Very simply, Captain Zhi Liu, known as Jenny Ling, was told to find Kang and kill him. Ji Wu was now to contact "Jenny" and give the orders. But he had to wait until 5 pm Beijing time or 9 am UK time. Between then he finalized the plan.

Jenny Ling was preparing a lesson for the college when her phone pinged; the message she read told her to contact Shizi. She opened her laptop, logged on, entered the chat room, and found Shizi.

He talked about what he wanted, that a weapon and ammunition would be provided, and that she would get help; contacts would be put in place. He told "Jenny" to go now to Edgefield, pick up the trail, and pick up the weapon that would be dropped at a certain point. She was also told her mission was of the utmost importance. She was not told that Kangs's treachery had not only wound up the British networks but also a New York one and a Washington one, both discovered when a British

A Chinese journalist revealed contacts in the US; having been threatened with being exchanged for a British agent in China, the journalist wanted to stay; the idea of the workers' paradise was not such a good idea.

"Jenny" had listened to Shizi, and then when finished, she packed a suitcase and left a note for Mrs. Dixon, her cleaner, and a note for Rosemary Marsh, her next-door neighbor, to keep an eye on the house and to feed Suki, her Siamese cat. Then she loaded the car up and drove off to join the hunt for Kang.

Just as "Jenny" was driving off, Horton and Harvey were discussing George Davies; he had been a topic since the explosive night with the chief constable. Now Harvey had decided to "bring him in" and find out what he knew. Horton was sent to get him.

CHAPTER 19

It was a beautiful early summer evening when George Davies was ushered into the living room at Edgefield. Harvey was sitting in an armchair with a bottle of wine, a bottle of whiskey, and two wine glasses and two whiskey glasses. "Help yourself." Harvey adjusted his position as Davies sat down opposite.

Pouring himself a glass of wine, Harvey kicked off. "Tell me what you know of Colonel Ling Kang, lately of the Ministry of State Security in China and now under our protection." Davies, who had poured himself a whiskey, stared in disbelief at the man opposite. He watched in wonder and fear as the man opposite stared at him with a blank, almost disconnected look, as Davies was being ignored. Davies answered, "I did not know he was who you say he was; I only knew he was a suspect in our hunt for a serial killer."

"You did not know of our interest." Harvey did not stop the stare. "No," repeated Davies. Harvey picked up the wine and drank. "You know the statute of limitations prevents the crimes in Hong Kong from being brought to trial." "I know, but this recent one he can be arrested for." Davies also stared, deciding to see if he could get a reaction. Harvey held his wine glass in his hand, the reflection of the room in the glass. "No, it won't happen. Kang is important for the security of the United Kingdom; he will be incarcerated but have no trial." "But what about the victims' family?" Davies felt he was losing the fight; he was right. "The family will be told what is necessary for them to know.". Davies looked disgusted. "No need to play the hurt one; we will deal with him, I promise." Davies listened, he thought and played his ace. He knew that Kang was on the run; he deliberately had not said anything, waiting for Harvey to make a stand. Harvey had; Davies did not like what he heard. He laid his case out: "When you recapture him.".

Harvey said nothing and did nothing after Davies had said his piece. Seconds passed, and Harvey broke the silence. " Alright, Mr. Davies, you said your piece; we will handle it for now." With that, Harvey pressed a button that was inset in the armrest of his chair, and Horton arrived. "Take Mr. Davies home, please." "Goodbye, Mr. Davies."

CHAPTER 20

Alonso was sitting at his kitchen table; his partner, Danny, had taken her sister's son to the zoo for the afternoon. She had asked James to come along, but he declined because he had a problem: it was that in the fuss and commotion of Kang, he had not had time to tell Harvey about Kang and his claim of a mole in SIS. Now,, he had to. He looked at his tea white with no sugar. He thought it was another English habit picked up during his time here, along with BBC radio and Rugby Union; he also found it fascinating that the British could play such a game with no armour on or helmet, unlike the NFL. His mind went back to the problem. The best thing was to ask for a meeting at Harvey's Mews place. He picked up the phone.

Kang was alert, nervous, and weary. He guessed it was about two days since his escape as he sat on a log in the woods of which he had no name; he followed the road and had found a hiding place now. He was under the same beautiful early summer evening that had seen Davies giving a lecture and Alonso wondering how to break bad news. Kang looked inside his bag for the remains of his supplies: a few slices of bread, two apples, and a little water. He knew he had to get more, and that meant using the card that meant it would register as used, and of course, that meant the authorities knew where he was, or roughly at least, but still he decided to eat, and Kang got off the log and decided to walk all summer night until he found a chance.

While Kang had started to walk, Jenny Li had arrived at her hotel near Edgefield; she had booked in and made her first contact. She had been told it was a woman in the restaurant. She had gone into the restaurant and found her contact, who had given her hold all. She had taken it back to her room and taken out the QBU-88 sniper rifle and ammunition. She had also been told that Kang was probably heading for London. She was ordered to stay put until Kang showed himself.

It was raining when Alonso reached the "Middle Mews." He got out of his car, and he saw Horton walking towards him. "Hi, Jimmy," Horton smiled at the American. "Fine," said the American. "and you?" "I'm good. I'm good. Let's see what the great leader wants.". They walked toward the front door of Harvey's home; they saw it open, and the "great leader" appeared. "Come in, come in; it's a bad day." Harvey led the way to the living room, "tea or coffee and something stronger if need be," Harvey pointed to the whiskey bottle. Horton took coffee, Alonso took tea, and Harvey took a coffee. The whiskey went back into the cabinet. "Ok, young Jimmy, what's the problem? You weren't very helpful on the phone."

Alonso sat in his armchair, teacup on the coffee table, and looking pensive. "Come on, James, out with it," Harvey encouraged the American, who finally said, "You have a mole in SIS.". "Who told you this?" Harvey leaned forward as if to make sure he understood what the American was saying. Alonso went on:" Kang told us that General Cheng had a mole, code name Robin." "You believe this?" Horton chipped in. "Yes, so far, everything we have asked has been answered and confirmed; he is a good witness." Harvey paused and, for a few seconds, seemed in deep thought; eventually, he said, "Ok, we have to find him.". The meeting broke up, and it was decided to meet at Edgefield next week.

Kang had been walking all night; at daybreak, the early morning sun shone bright, welcoming another bright day and giving Kang his first chance. He saw a coffee shop on the roadside with a full car park and a cash machine just inside the entrance. Kang went inside and withdrew a thousand pounds. He then went to get breakfast.

At that moment, in the fraud section of the Northern Associated Bank, the AI picked up the card use, and a message was sent; within minutes, Thomas Nixon, the duty officer, had contacted the police and told them where the card had been used. He also told his former boss, Robert Horton, as a favor repaid.

Kang had finished his breakfast; he paid and in paying had found out there was a Premier Inn just down the road. He figured he had a night before he moved on again, so he started walking; it had been a 30-minhad been, he had been told. He started. But he was not alone; he had failed to notice the elderly man sitting, also having breakfast.

George Davies could not believe his eyes; he had been on his way back to Edgefield to try and find Kang himself. Now,, his prey had walked into the same cafe! He had watched Kang and thought about what to do. He saw Kang leave; he went up to the counter and, with great charm, persuaded eighteen-year-old Emma, the cashier, to tell him what she had told Kang. Davies waited about half an hour and then drove for Hare Field.

Horton found the message left from Dixon on his desk; he was pleased he had remembered the former officer, now paralysed, and he alerted Harvey and Alonso. Harvey had asked Horton where he thought Kang was heading; Horton guessed the next village, Hare Field. Harvey had then told

Horton to send someone to check to see if Kang was there. In the meantime, a photograph was issued to the police; the media was not informed, as Kang had avoided populations and not been seen, and now there was a chance to end it quietly, and Horton decided to send Simpson as the "observer," as Kang would know Jimmy and Roger. He rang Simpson and asked for a meeting.

CHAPTER 21

"Well, that is it then. You are to go to Hare Field and see if he is there, watch him, and report anything suspicious. We booked you a room." Horton finished his brief, and Simpson sat quietly and listened. "What if he moves?" Simpson asked, "Follow him," was the short, pointed reply. With that, Simpson got up and started to move towards the door. "Have got everything you need for a night's stay." Horton thought he better ask, "Yes, I have always had a suitcase in the car. "Good, "Horton was relieved. He wished Simpson good luck.

Outside, Simpson got into his car and made a phone call over WhatsApp: "It's a nice day to go to the zoo and see the lions. "Simpson hoped he would get the reply he expected; he did: "Nice day to birdwatch, especially robins," the owner of the voice continued: "What have you got for me?" Simpson told the voice that belonged to Shizi everything. At the other end of the world, Ji Wu listened and then said, "Do these things contact this person?" Wu gave him "Jennys," or Zhi Liu, contact details, telling him to take instructions from her. Simpson agreed; the call ended, and Simpson rang Ling as he wanted to know her. The phone call lasted 10 minutes. It was agreed that Ling would arrive and Simpson would do his bit, but he was to act like a stranger with any Asian woman he might meet. Simpson agreed, put the phone down, and drove to Hare Field.

Alonso was angry, angry at being told to stay out of the hunt. True, he thought it was a British operation, but from a personal point of view, it was the CIA—the people who paid him—who had told the British cousins that their golden prize was a serial killer. He wanted to be on the hunt, but Harvey, in true British fashion, had told Alonso, very politely, to "fuck off. Alonso remembered what he said:

"Sorry, Jimmy Kang knows you can't have him around. Come to Edgefield when we bring him in." Alonso sat and just thought about getting angry every second. He was about to let some energy out when he had an idea; perhaps it would work...

George Davies pulled into the car park of the hotel. He looked at his watch; it said 4 minutes past ten. He thought and figured that Kang was twenty minutes behind. He collected his bag, went inside, and booked in. The receptionist told him they were virtually empty; this was good news, Davies thought. He got to his hotel room, unpacked, and settled down; fortunately, his room overlooked the car park and front door, so he could see who was coming and going.

He did not have to wait long; sure enough, just over twenty minutes after he had got there, Kang turned up, booked in, and asked about washing his clothes. He was told he missed that day's service, but tomorrow, if he could, by ten in the morning, his clothes would be ready. Kang agreed, as he still had a pair of jeans and a T-shirt left to wear. He went to his room; at that moment, the door swung open, and in walked a man and woman. The woman was Chinese. As Kang was moving, he heard the man call himself "Simpson." Kang went to his room. In his room,; Davies had seen the arrivals, too. The man had no idea, but the woman worried him; two Chinese in the same hotel, naturally it was possible, but given the present circumstances, there was a strong possibility these two had a connection; he just had to think about it, but that needed time, and time was something he not have.

At Edgefield, Horton had taken a call from Simpson, just reporting that he had arrived with no sign of Kang and all was quiet. Horton was told to report as soon as he knew anything about anything.

So, the day dragged on. Simpson, Kāng, Davies, and Liu, three of them, waited for the evening and a chance to see if their target was there; the fourth needed a bed and time to think.

Kang lay on the bed deep in thought, the first being he needed to shave; he could have let the beard grow, but he was not too keen on facial hair, believing it was not his style. His second and more important thought was hotel layout; he had noticed that as you entered the hotel, the reception desk was right in front of you. To the left was a door leading to the rooms, and a door to the right led to the small bar lounge. The restaurant was a separate building; you had to come out of the hotel, walk across the car park, and through a gate down a path to the Wayside In, which was the hotel restaurant as well as a roadside cafe.

In the restaurant, at the far end, was the fire escape. Kang decided to eat at the table nearest to the fire exit so he could escape quickly in the event of an emergency. Kang thought further; how was he going to get further? He had money, so a taxi would be a good idea; the driver may recognise him, but that was a chance that must be taken. Kang looked at his watch; nearly three in the afternoon, he lay on the bed, shut his eyes, and rested.

Kang may not have been recognized by a taxi driver but had been recognised by the receptionist Lucy. Lucy had been in a quandary since seeing Kang; she thought it was the fugitive in the newspaper but could not be sure. However, she had swallowed her fears and rung the number in the newspaper and spoke to a woman who took the details and told her not to worry; it would be sorted out. Lucy was relieved; she put the phone down. At the other end of the line, Mrs. Donaldson contacted Robert Horton, who happened to be out with Harvey having lunch. She told him, "Independent sighting; he's there all right." Horton was relieved Simpson had not seen anything yet, and now he had a sighting. He turned to Harvey, "We have a sighting; the receptionist saw him." "Good, well, I suggest we finish lunch and then get the show on the road. I will request armed police help." "What about the SAS?" Horton queried. "No, absolute no; you forget Kang does not exist and should exist. We have the army here, and we have a circus show, media, the lot—no, plain, simple, and quiet." "Now, suggest the chocolate pie for dessert." Harvey started eating again, leaving Horton bemused.

Zhi Liu was looking at the hotel plan with fire exits that adorned each hotel room door. She had planned to use the sniper's rifle, but now, with Kang this close, that would no longer work; when she struck, it would have to be face-to-face. She looked at what she had, a knife and a pistol with a silencer. She decided to kill him in his room after supper. She thought she would try to get to know him and lead him on, and then back in his room she would strike. She also had plan B, which would be the room service plan: trick her way in and then...

Horton and Harvey had finished lunch and were now back at Edgefield in a Zoom meeting with the Chief Constable. "Well, there it is, Jonathan; that's the plan: we grab Kang at the hotel tomorrow morning in his room." Harvey waited for a response, "We grab him in the carpark; he needs to move on. If we catch him in his room, we will have to go inside; that could mean innocent bystanders hurt if he resists; better outside." "OK, outside," Harvey gave way. Horton interjected, "How many officers?" "I fix that." Michaels was already assigning people to the task in his head. "Well then, until tomorrow, first light, and hope good hunting." Harvey closed the meeting.

The time was six in the evening, the Zoom meeting ended, and in a restaurant, four people were taking up their table positions. Kang had his table alone, Simpson was at the other end also alone, and a Chinese woman had ended up with an elderly British man. Kang scanned the lot.

CHAPTER 22

Kang had scanned the room. There were ten people there; the first three were young men coming back from a party and discussing one of the women they had met, and the next three were a family coming back from a seaside holiday that left an old man who Kang had noticed had been watching him, Kang, probably just out of curiosity, but as Kang thought best to keep a distance. That left the last two, and Kang paid special attention.

The first one was a man, a redhead with a beard. He was tall, about one meter ninety tall, and well-muscled, army type, thought Kang, but still there was something Kang was worried about; he had a memory somehow of the man but could not place it. He watched the woman; like him, she was Chinese, and she had a business-type look. She wore an above-knee skirt and a white blouse; her hair was back in a ponytail. Like the man, she looked familiar, but the memory was not there. Kang tried to place it but could not. He did notice, however, that she took care of herself, as she seemed to have well-muscled legs and arms. Kang decided that she had to be avoided.

Supper went slowly, and Kang, while eating, kept his eyes and ears open and heard or saw nothing to cause alarm. He thought about it after supper, drinking a coffee. Perhaps he should go to his room; he'd be safe there and could defend himself if attacked. He looked at the woman again. He really had a bad gut feeling. He decided he needed thinking time, and to do that, he needed to look and remember. He decided to go to the bar; getting up from his table, he saw the woman was moving. He went toward the door, opened it, and went through; at the same time, the woman caught up, and he held it open. "Thank you." "No problem," he replied; he noticed the woman had replied in faultless British English. "Nice night for a walk. I'm on my way to London." Kang told a truth amongst his many, many lies. "I'm visiting friends." The woman walked beside him; he noticed perfume, very nice, and he liked her figure, but there was the memory. Kang then made his move, "I'm going for a drink; care to join me?" "Yes." The woman agreed, and soon, they were sitting down and making small talk. They talked and lied willingly to each other; Kang offered to buy drinks. The woman wanted red wine.

Kang went to the bar and ordered; while waiting, he cast his eyes over to a TV screen. It showed a news report about North Korea and some big military parade. He looked and saw female soldiers in uniform. It was his cathartic moment; his mind, like an old sixteen-millimeter projector, began spinning, and he saw in his mind's eye a sports hall with General Cheng and a new recruit. Cheng had said she was the best agent ever during training, and she had just done an "Illegals" course.

Cheng said she could speak British English, American English, French, and German as foreign languages; she was artistic as well, but most importantly, she was a real professional when it came to combat skills. Cheng had waxed lyrical; she was dangerous, very dangerous. Kang remembered now Zhi Liu; that was her name, and she was here, sitting in the bar. Kang knew why she was here; he thought quickly, should he leave? But that was a bad idea; he had no transport, and she did. She could catch up with him, and if she had to follow over the countryside, she could do that too. So, he decided to stay put and go in the morning. Kang's mind was spinning with thought after thought, as water from a flowing tap went through his head. Just then, he saw the red-bearded man. His mind's projector started up, and he remembered him too, Simpson; he remembered Cheng had told him of a SIS man recruited in Britain, a real communist sympathizer, a man called Simpson and given the code name Robin.

He went back to the table. "I don't feel well; it must have been the food," he lied. Zhi Liu looked at him with a smile that did hide the disappointment of not being able to finish him tonight. She said,

"Goodnight then, and tomorrow, if you want, I could give you a lift to London; I'm leaving after breakfast." Kang thought that meant she would be leaving between eight and nine; that would give him time to order a taxi; seven would be a good time. "Ok, I would like that," he lied. "See you in the morning," Zhi Liu also lied. She guessed what he was planning, and she would be waiting.

"Well, that's the plan," Jonathan Micheals laid the plan before the party assembled. "Can we go through it once again so we can be sure?" Harvey was looking pensive; he was now beginning to double-check everything.

Micheals put a handmade map and a model of the car park on the table. "We will be in cover here, he pointed to a hedge on the left of the car park, and we will have a second position here on the right amongst the cars when Kang comes out; we grab him." That simple, "Horton chipped in. "Well, it is the fastest and best chance for a capture; early in the morning, from six in the morning, we will be waiting. Micheals sounded confident. "Is Kang still there?" Micheals quickly added. "Yes, Simpson reported in. He is not moving,"

Horton sounded confident. "How many officers again?"
Harvey looked at the table: "Eight, four in each position."
Micheals prepared for the next question, but there was none.
Harvey just nodded his approval, and the party broke up.

Zhi Liu had her plan; Kang was going to leave before
she did, but she guessed he needed transport and food, so he
would be gone by seven, say, or maybe later, but she would
be around. Unfortunately, the rifle plan was now useless, but
she was armed. She decided to pack the car that night so she
could escape quickly.

Davies had decided to make his move; he would make a
citizen's arrest, so he called the police and told them he had
found the policewoman's killer. The dispatcher at the other
end made a note of what Davies had said, and then she, as
instructed when dealing with this suspect, sent an email to a
place called Edgefield. Horton picked it up and showed it to
Micheals, who said simply, "We have it anyway; Davies does
not matter.". Horton looked at the clock. At eleven pm, the
police would move in at five in the morning.

The sun rose at four minutes past five in the morning.
Micheals and the two SIS officers were parked on the road
outside the hotel. The van was marked "Edgefield Plumber,"
one of the observation vans used by the SIS. Inside it was
equipped with listening equipment and cameras and video
cameras.

Harvey was watching; he was getting agitated. Perhaps
Kang had gone, but the receptionist had said no one had left,
and to prove the point, she had shown a detective constable
the CCTV. The officer had reported this to the van, and
everyone relaxed. Horton looked at his watch; it said twenty-
past-five. He looked at the chief constable. "Your men

ready?" "Yes," Micheals responded. "Well, it is up to Kang now," Harvey was thinking aloud.

Another five minutes passed, and in the hotel, Kang was waking up. He shaved, showered, and got dressed. He went out into the hallway and ran into Zhi Liu. "Good morning." "Good morning." They both almost spoke at once; they gave false smiles, knowing what was really going to happen.

On the way to breakfast, Kang made small talk.

"Yes," came the blunt and disinterested reply.

Both walked to the dining room, and Kang saw his chance to book his taxi.

"I need to grab my wallet; I want to pay this morning and leave right after I've eaten," he said.

Zhi Liu watched and nodded as Kang went through the door and returned to the hotel. She waited two minutes, got up, and went to the door and then to the hotel; she did not go in but stayed at the entrance, pretending to read the tourist literature on a bookshelf. She was watching Kang and listening to the receptionist, "Yes sir, seven, a taxi I can book that." Zhi Liu went back to the restaurant looked at her watch, six twenty; she finished her coffee and toast and went to prepare. The time was six thirty-five.

As she went out, Davies came in; he looked at the woman and wondered where Kang was; he also wondered where the police were; perhaps they already had him in custody. He started to eat.

The time was six forty. Zhi Liu was prepared; the type 67 pistol with an inbuilt silencer was in a shoulder holster, ready. She rehearsed; Kang would come out, and she would follow.

Kang would open the taxi door, and she would open fire. The time was six forty-five.

She heard the footsteps and waited; her watch said six forty-eight. She went into the hallway; Kang was settling the bill with the receptionist, and she waited. Kang paid and started to move toward the door; the time was six fifty-two. Zhi Liu watched as she saw the taxi and saw Kang; he went through the door, and she followed, ready. At that moment, George Davies appeared and saw Kang; he looked and shouted, "Hey, you stop!" Zhi Liu pointed the pistol, and Kang swung around as though he sensed her; then they both heard, "Armed police, drop the weapon." Zhi Liu reacted and pulled the trigger twice; then she heard another shot; the next thing she felt was a thud in her head, and then the blackness overtook her.

"They are both dead, sir." The uniformed sergeant looked over the bodies; Kang was in the taxi, and two bullets had exploded in his chest. The sergeant explained the bullets were dum dum, exploding on impact. The unknown woman was dead on the floor at the entrance, a single bullet hole between the eyes. Micheals looked at the body. "Excellent shot," he commented. He then noticed Davies and the taxi driver both in a state of shock. Harvey went to Davies. "It's over; he is dead. Your and our work is over," Davies said nothing; he just stood. Harvey turned to Horton. "You know what to do with the bodies.".

A few hours later, Micheals, Harvey, Horton, Davies, and Alonso were at Edgefield. Harvey started the proceedings: "In view of today's events, it seems we can close the Alpha File as Alpha is dead." Davies looked at him, "That's right; we used the file and names; thought it was easier." Harvey turned to Alonso. "Thank you for your cooperation. We will, of course, provide your people with the information discovered." Alonso stared; he had been told by Langley to stay out; he was angry but accepted the "fait accompli." Horton said, "Who was the woman?" No one knew, and investigations turned up very little.

Harvey looked at the party, "I think that's all now. Thank you for your attention in this matter.". With that, the party broke up. Colonel Lin Kang was in espionage history; Captain Zhi Liu remained a mystery.

The End